31 HOURS

**Center Point
Large Print**

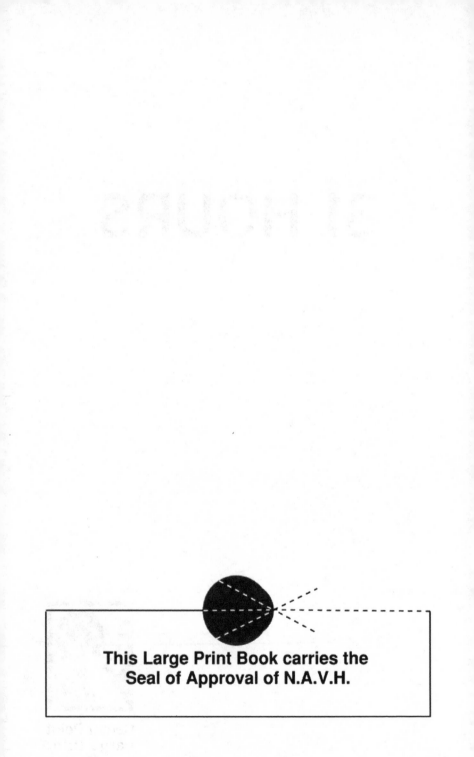

**This Large Print Book carries the
Seal of Approval of N.A.V.H.**

31 HOURS

MASHA HAMILTON

CENTER POINT PUBLISHING
THORNDIKE, MAINE

This Center Point Large Print edition
is published in the year 2010 by arrangement with
Unbridled Books.

The text of this Large Print edition is unabridged.
In other aspects, this book may vary
from the original edition.
Printed in the United States of America
on permanent paper.
Set in 16-point Times New Roman type.

ISBN: 978-1-60285-821-3

Library of Congress Cataloging-in-Publication Data

Hamilton, Masha.
  31 hours / Masha Hamilton.
      p. cm.
  ISBN 978-1-60285-821-3 (library binding : alk. paper)
  1. Terrorists—Fiction. 2. Mothers and sons—Fiction. 3. New York (N.Y.)—Fiction.
  4. Large type books. I. Title. II. Title: Thirty-one hours.
  PS3558.A44338A615 2010
  813′.54—dc22
                                                    2010006777

To the mothers:
Arra Kulinovich Hamilton,
Frankie Mayfield Kulinovich,
Jesse Crilly Hamilton

I think we should maybe have the courage to identify ourselves with and humanize the torturer. Maybe we should look at ourselves, instead of saying "never again," which does not work. We could maybe try to ask a new question, as well as a very old one: "How is it possible?" We may find the answers in ourselves.

—François Bizot,
ethnologist captured
by the Khmer Rouge
in 1971 and author of the
memoir The Gate

And everything
and nothing
is as sacred as we want it to be.
—Beth Orton,
"Central Reservation" lyrics

NEW YORK: 1:44 A.M.
MECCA: 9:44 A.M.

A wolf's howl. But more shrill, more prolonged. Carol sat fully upright, an inhale caught in her chest, before she realized there was, of course, no rabid wolf dodging Manhattan traffic. It was only winter's wind slicing past her eleventh-floor apartment window with enough ferocity to rouse her. Then she grasped, in quick succession, that she'd been half-awake before the noise began, that her stomach hurt, and that her mind was filled with Jonas. Her son. Her wild-haired precious. When he was tiny, on a frenzied night like this, he would have snuggled with her in this very bed, bare toes pressing against her leg. Now he extended over six feet, and though he hugged, he didn't snuggle. God, where had those days gone?

More important: Where was he now?

She lay back down, reached to pull a pillow close, and smoothed her forehead with a hand as if wiping dust from a table. She wondered if she could will herself back to sleep but doubted it. Her most successful years of slumber stretched from Jonas's birth through his toddlerhood, when the basics felt simple and pure and her arms had been full of husband and baby, potter's clay and home-made bread. Through the remaining, darker days of marriage, divorce, and the occasional lover, erratic sleep became the status quo. Still, whenever she awakened in the wee hours, she wanted nothing more than to breathe in time with another human body—a desire that pointed to a primitive quality in her, she thought, one not suited to this modern life. At age forty-eight, she still wasn't used to sleeping alone.

When Jake was already gone and Jonas still a boy, she would sometimes crawl into her young son's bed, rest a hand on his tummy, and match her breath to his. Often, if her presence woke him—she hadn't thought of this in years—he would lull himself back to sleep by twirling her hair with his fingers, as if they were joined. He was so small then that air passed through his body at a pace more urgent than soothing. But the rise and fall of his stomach connected her to nothing less than the universe itself. Jonas saved her from facing her own mortality during those long nights. Next to him, imagining herself a kite finally cut free of its string, she slept.

That perfect boy with his drowsy warm scent and hair falling on the pillow like a piece of art. Why hadn't he returned her calls?

But why should that be such a big deal? At twenty-one, separating from parents and establishing one's individuality was a desired, even critical, stage. "Differentiation" was the term, wasn't it? She had to give him space, trust him. That's what it meant to be the parent of a grown child.

Well, screw differentiation. Screw psychobabble that blurred the particularities of Carol and her son and her mother-intuition. He'd always been so sensitive, before. He would never have wanted her to feel this scared, and if he wouldn't—or couldn't—pick up the phone to ease her anxiety now, that only proved it. Something was wrong.

She massaged her scalp for a moment and then squeezed her eyes closed, trying to picture Jonas in his Greenwich Village apartment. She failed. She tried to envision him in a lecture hall at NYU. That didn't work, either. A hospital bed in Midtown? Sunk to the bottom of the East River?

Oh, God. Night-fed fears; she knew all about them. Keep this up, and shadows would become serial killers hiding beneath the bed. She was as unreasonable as a child awakened from a nightmare, she told herself, but that thought, though reassuring, felt unconvincing. This must be what it meant to worry oneself sick—although this emotion seemed closer to premonition, which made it even more alarming. Simple worry she could dismiss as wisps of weariness-fueled nonsense. Portent was born of concrete facts not yet processed by the conscious mind.

She threw her arm over her face. *Be rational,* she instructed herself. *Put it into words: I am worried because . . .*

Because Jonas recently had seemed so troubled. Too vulnerable, too raw, even for him. Too prone to anger that would rise like a wind gust and then die as swiftly. Too distant—perhaps that most of all. The heaviness she'd been feeling in her limbs for days *could* be dismissed as some delayed empty-nest response. But what if it was caused by something larger? What if her past with her baby, her boy, hadn't simply evolved as it was supposed to with one's grown children? What if, somehow, all those moments and memories laid in place like bricks used to build a house had vanished entirely, become dust while she'd been looking the other way?

A pipe moaned in the walls, while out in the hallway the elevator lumbered to life. On the icy streets below, on a night like this, cars careened with vulnerability, bakers lingered close to their ovens, and subways grumbled on their tracks as they rushed young partygoers and workers just off night shifts to their homes. She rolled onto her stomach and buried her nose and mouth in the pillow until she had to turn her cheek to the side to breathe. Breathe, she told herself. Rest, and soften the shoulders, and stop the mind's see-sawing, at least until dawn. Yes, dawn. And then, young adult or not, she would track him down. She would touch his cheek and hug him tight—mother him until he shrugged her off—so the next time night fell, she could hold assurance close to her like a childhood blanket and rest with the vigor of the innocent and the blessed.

Tile.

Cool, powder-blue tile, chipped in places and hard against his bare feet.

And a razor with an orange handle. A package of them, actually. Ten in all.

Bathroom tile and drugstore razors.

Bathroom tile and drugstore razors.

Bathroom tile and drugstore razors.

It was a prayer.

That wasn't such a preposterous idea—anything could be a prayer. Should be, in fact. Every step Jonas took, every idle thought that eased through his head: a holy, ongoing dialogue with God. Or perhaps a plea, because at this moment, he shouldn't be chatting with God as though they were dinner partners. He needed to be a supplicant. *Please. Please give me the brains to remember what I've been taught and, please, the speed to do it quickly. And the calm, so that I can avoid undue attention and accomplish what I need to accomplish. Mercy, too. Have mercy, please, oh God, on my soul.*

Allah, rather. Allah, for God's sake. Allah. Get with the program.

Unexpectedly amused by his own private stumblings over his Creator's proper name—or name in proper context—and pleased that he still *had* the capacity to be amused, Jonas smiled faintly at himself in the mirror. His skin looked even paler than usual under the fluorescent light, smoky-white and artificial, and it merged seamlessly into the ash-blond hair that stood out on his head in waves of thick curls. Ridiculous hair, really. Locks that little boys have but then outgrow, only he never did. Women loved his Jewfro. Always had. When he was twelve, that friend of his mother's poked her fingers into his tangle of hair and he'd seen her eyes go foggy and he'd realized even then that she was fantasizing—perhaps not about him, exactly, not about her friend's little boy, not that—but still some fantasy that was loose and sensual, arising from the way his long hair twisted out from his head and the way her fingers felt, vanished among the silky strands. It had surprised him, scared him, really, and later angered him. He sensed something predatory in it, something that failed to take him into account at all. And when he mentioned it to his mother—his bohemian, touchy-feely, let's-talk-about-it mother—she'd pulled away as if he'd slapped her and said he was wrong; her friend had known him since he was in diapers, since he made "doodies" (that was the way she talked) and she'd had to wipe him clean.

And that was enough, more than enough, to end that conversation forever. As she'd no doubt intended.

Jonas sat on the toilet and stretched his long legs, already stripped of their jeans. He hadn't been able to sleep, had been sleeping poorly for months, in fact. So he might as well begin the process now. He knew the drill, this part of it, anyway. He had to purify himself. That was step one. Purify by removing all hair except for the curls on his head; they'd told him to leave those for later. Then pray toward Mecca. Then eat if he wanted, or fast if he chose, either option permissible, Masoud had said. Then pray and purify even more. Later, Masoud would bring the clean clothes and the Qur'an, which Jonas would place in his right-hand pocket. How did it go? Something old, something new. Something borrowed . . .

He twisted his torso to pick up his digital camera from the top of the toilet tank. He intended to document each step along the way so the pictures could be there for someone to look at later, and maybe understand. He had an idea, loosely formed, that he would want to be understood, if there was any wanting left on the other side. He hoped candid shots of him preparing might illustrate his foresight as well as his determination, because the news reports would surely flatten him to a two-dimensional zealot. He'd be seen as naive—mad, maybe. Someone might accuse him of being a crackhead, though he never used drugs and rarely drank. Others would be perplexed, especially people who were able to overlook evil and lose themselves in their own narrow lives. They'd find it hard to figure out why he couldn't just ignore, too. Those who could identify with his anguish over the way things were would probably be unwilling to admit it aloud for fear of being seen as sympathizing with a nut-job. Deirdre might be the only person who would really understand, though he'd lost touch with her long ago. How long?

Jonas snapped a photograph and glanced at his wristwatch. Seven minutes to 2. In seven more minutes, it would be—he used his fingers—thirty-one hours until.

Thirty-one.

The maximum number of days in a month, the length between menstrual cycles. Al-Khabir, the All-Aware, the thirty-first name of Allah. Thirty-one verses in Genesis, Chapter 1. The thirty-first verse: *God saw all that he had made, and behold, it was very good. It was evening and it was morning, the sixth day.* Thirty-one hours which, given the elasticity of time, could shrink to thirty-one seconds or expand to thirty-one years. Who knew what the next thirty-one hours would feel like to him? And then he snapped a picture of his legs, hairy, with knotty apple-knees. Men's legs, in general, aren't very attractive, though they are functional and it's more important to be useful than attractive.

There it was: another prayer.

More important to be useful than attractive, oh Allah.

Jewish dad, atheist mom, raised faithless, Jonas had, despite that, grown adept at spotting prayers.

He perched on the ledge of the bathtub, swinging his legs around and in as he picked up the can of mint-scented gel. He shook it, and sprayed some on his right ankle, spreading it upward until his leg turned white—almost gleaming under the insistent lighting—and he wondered how it would feel to be made of snow, and to reflect brightness, and to fear nothing except the sun. Then he carefully removed the cover from the first razor. He felt a bit clumsy, taking that initial swipe on the right side of his calf near his ankle. Was it uncontrolled nervousness or simply unfamiliarity? He had the advantage of being pretty hairless to start with. In fact, he shaved his stubble only twice a week. He'd always hated how his smooth cheeks made him look younger than he was.

Jonas turned on the water so he could rinse the razor as he went. The tub's enamel was chipped, and a streak of rust reached out from the drain like an orange cobweb. In another time and another part of Manhattan, he used to put dirty dishes in his apartment's bathtub if he knew his mother was dropping by. He would pile them up and close the shower curtain. Later he would have to move the dishes back to the kitchen and, eventually, wash them. So if you thought about it, it was really more work in the end, but still he enjoyed it, fooling his mom. Or so he thought until the day she called to say she'd be stopping by that afternoon and added, a lilt in her voice, "and I'll be wanting to take a bath."

He put the blade to his calf and let the sharp metal graze the surface, felling coarse hair as it went, leaving behind naked flesh. Despite his intense concentration, he noticed the subway passing nearby, causing the bathroom wall to vibrate. It was the J, or maybe the M. He wasn't that familiar with the City Hall district. Jonas had grown up on the Upper West Side and had attended an artsy high school in Midtown and then NYU. He felt surprisingly like a foreigner over here, where the bridges stretched longingly toward Brooklyn and he could buy a pack of disposable razors in a store called Confucius Pharmacy. "Say it again?" he'd asked when Masoud had told him that the studio apartment where he would stay was right off the Avenue of the Finest. A street praising the diligence of New York City cops. He'd never heard of it. He felt sure Masoud was joking. And although the street did exist, it *was* a joke of sorts. A creepy, haunting joke the media might pick up on, afterward. But they'd be busy with other distractions, so maybe they wouldn't, and that didn't matter because by then it would have taken on all the intimacy of a private joke for the benefit of Masoud.

And Jonas felt fine with that. He did.

After a few swipes, he angled the razor under the running water and shaved more and then more, dulling two razors before the right calf felt smooth to his touch, a girl's leg. Next he spread shaving cream on his shin, where the bone strained against the skin. This part, he knew, was a bit trickier; this was where women often nicked themselves. He knew this because Vic had told him. About a month ago, he'd asked her what was the worst thing about shaving and she'd laughed one of her short, husky laughs that made him ache with longing and said, "You ask the damnedest questions, Jonas."

"But just tell me," he insisted. "Like, the first time you ever shaved. What was the worst part?" He was already thinking about today.

So she'd told him. She'd sprawled on her couch, flung a leg on his lap. "My shinbone," she'd said; "this part here," and she'd taken his fingers and placed them at her ankle and then drawn them slowly up her dancer's leg, over that bone so intimate with her cool, smooth flesh, and then beyond her knee, directly toward her heart, and she'd stopped midthigh, her smile wicked, her tone challenging, and teased: "Is your curiosity satisfied, boy?"

God, he would miss her. If missing is possible, afterward. What he felt was so intense, even more intense than with Deirdre. He thought now of changing his mind, running away somewhere to hide until he could figure out how to tell them it was off. That would be the way of a coward, though. That would be throwing everything out: the training, the commitment. He'd already made *baty al-ridwan*, a pledge not to waver. Besides, though Vic had heightened his joy, she'd also increased his suffering. She'd stopped calling, and it wasn't a surprise. He was a loner; he'd always been a loner; that was the way life had gone for him. He'd known from the start that someone as solid and wonderful as Vic would eventually weary of his intensity and mood swings and move on, forgetting him.

This way, he would never be forgotten.

The bathroom suddenly felt airless. What would Masoud advise? Don't think of her would be his counsel. "This kind of personal attachment is not indicated for us," Jonas imagined him saying. Remember the lessons that must be taught, the sins that must be atoned for. Seek refuge from hypocrisy, and from the love of this world. Remember your good fortune in having been chosen. That was always his mantra, one Jonas did still believe. He knew what had to be reversed, and why and how. He recognized a will and wisdom greater than his own. The personal wasn't paramount. He was acting out of an obligation larger than himself.

Jonas thought of a line from the Qur'an. *O Prophet! Strive hard against the Unbelievers and the Hypocrites, and be firm against them, their abode is Hell—an evil refuge indeed.* Sura 9:73. He chanted the line a few times, then added a little extra shaving gel to his leg and, holding his breath, carefully began to draw the razor up against the delicate shinbone. After the first sweep, he exhaled. So far, so good. No blood. No blood yet. No blood and—he tested with a pointed finger—slick as a whale. Why had he thought of a whale? He didn't know, except that he remembered being told that story countless times in childhood, about Jonas in the belly of the whale. Besides, a whale was strong and vigorous, and that was what he wanted to be: slick, and strong, and headed for purity.

"Hey, Hirt. Wake up, Sonny, c'mon." The cop rapped his nightstick on the base of the subway seat, and Sonny Hirt, slouched on his right side with the graffiti-etched window for a pillow, squinted open one reluctant brown eye.

"Officer," he said in a phlegmy voice, then cleared his throat. "How you be?"

"You know the drill, Hirt. No vagrants sleeping on the subway. Move it."

"Vagrant? What you mean, officer?" Sonny Hirt allowed for an indignant tone as he sat up, stifling a yawn. "And I ain't sleeping. Wouldn't be safe, sleep here."

"Uh-huh."

"That's right. I just takin' a little commercial break before game time."

"Sure."

"Or a chat at the water cooler, you could be calling it. Man who works on Sundays be entitled to a little breather. By the way," Sonny rubbed one stubbly cheek, "can you spare any?" Even half-conscious, he slipped into his shtick so easily; he was a master, a preacher with purpose, if he did say so himself. "If you ain't got it, I understand, 'cause I ain't got it. But if you have a dime, a quarter, a piece of fruit—"

"C'mon, c'mon. On your feet," the cop interrupted.

Sonny sat up and groaned, though he wasn't unhappy to be cut short. He wasn't quite ready to start spinning yet, anyway. He pulled his fingers through his mustache and beard. "Bones gettin' too old for this job," he said. "Gonna have to retire soon, move myself to Puerto Rico. Then you gonna be missing me."

"Hmmm," said the cop, though he smiled a little. Sonny didn't know him well enough to remember his name, but all the cops knew Sonny Hirt; lots of the regular commuters did, too. He'd been panhandling on these subway lines for nearly a decade now. Some of the teenagers who got on at Jay Street or Canal he remembered from when they were tots. These days they rode without their mommas, and they called him Mr. Hirt, and they laughed, but it wasn't mean laughter. How could anyone take offense at Sonny, who shuffled up and down the subway cars, politely doing his job, delivering his familiar spiel? The riders sure didn't mind, and the cops cut him slack, mostly speaking, if they caught him taking a little nap during downtime.

Every now and then, some newcomer in blue with a shiny nose and water sitting back of the ears would come down on him a bit. Shoo him away. Tell him he couldn't, wasn't allowed, a public nuisance. Even threaten to ticket him, usually in a loud, attention-getting voice. And what trouble was Sonny causing, after all? He was doing a job. A public service, if you thought of it, because it allowed folks to feel a little better about themselves as they headed toward whatever sins awaited them. Used to be, when the cops toyed with him, heat would shoot through Sonny's body from head to heels, like the Long Island expressway running right through him, and he'd have to work to keep his hands still and the fire clean from his eyes. Their smug looks, the conviction that they were better than ol' Sonny—when after all, real criminals were right aboveground slitting throats and selling drugs to kids. Besides, this was *his* place, the subway; *they* were the visitors.

But less and less was bothering Sonny as the years went on.

"Knew me a little Puerto Rican girl once," he told the cop now. "Mmm-mmm. She were quiet, but she could move." He rubbed his scalp underneath his yellow ski cap. "Them days," he said.

"Uh-huh," the cop said.

"Should'a stayed with that girl, but you know how it is. Tough for a man like me to be giving up the freelance and be committing to a steady life, that's what she always said, and I guess she were right some."

"Uh-huh."

"Coraly. Sweet Coraly." He shook his head,

feeling a pit in his stomach that came either from remembering Coraly or from hunger. "Sounds like I made her up, but she were real, all right," he said, tugging the ski cap down to cover more of his ears.

"Here's real for you," the cop said. "Don't let me catch you sleeping on the subway again. Not any day, but especially not today. Not today, Hirt. Ain't no halfway house for the homeless, and we're on alert, so follow the rules."

"Tell me, officer," Sonny said, "you ever have your own Coraly? The one so good it hurts to remember? Who might'a changed everything if you'da realized in time?" The cop didn't speak, but his expression changed from a man sucking a lemon slice to one with honey on his tongue. "Maybe that's something we all had," Sonny said as the train pulled into the Broadway-Lafayette station. "We all just human, after all."

As he headed out of the car, the cop held the subway door and turned back to Sonny, his voice slightly gentler. "Hope you were listening. Don't get your ass in trouble, not today." Then he stepped off, one hand slapping his holster, the thumb of the other stuck into his belt.

"Stand clear of the closing doors, please," a computerized woman's voice intoned.

As the doors slid shut, Sonny breathed in the contained subway air. Now that the cop mentioned it, Sonny could see that the place felt off balance, unusually tense. What most folks didn't know about Sonny was that he had this certain awareness. Sometimes when a man or lady handed Sonny a quarter or two, just as their hands grazed his, the world seemed to grow hushed and then some vision appeared in place of their faces or an odd scent would command the atmosphere. It meant something gone, or about to be.

Every time it happened, Sonny would shudder and shake his head—he didn't want to know more. He'd have to move on, quick, without his usual "God bless." Otherwise the image would stop him in his tracks. Trying to voice a warning would be useless, might even get him arrested. But the feeling came on so strong sometimes that he couldn't work the rest of that day. He'd go to a coffee shop where they knew him and nurse a cuppa, wrapping his fingers around the thick white mug until they stopped shaking.

Yes, his chosen profession had its bad days, even given its relative freedom. One of the worst parts, besides the premonitions, was running up against so many folks busy putting out dissatisfaction, or anger, or fear—all fueled by some surplus or absence of longing. Sonny had developed a theory about longing. In moderate doses, it was healthy, like a bit of salt sprinkled on a good meal. But too little meant a person had given up on life, while too much turned a body mad and desperate. If the passengers Sonny passed on any given day were filled with what he thought of as a longing imbalance, an anxious buzz began ringing in his ears. Sometimes he developed food-poisoning symptoms, turned dizzy and sick to his stomach. He wished he weren't so sensitive, but there it sat.

Other drawbacks were more mundane. Train delays, for instance. Some were scheduled, such as track work. Others fell in his way unplanned, like four or five weeks ago, when somebody dropped with a heart attack on the subway train ahead of them, bringing them to a halt for a good half-hour. And there stood Sonny, trapped in a single car, tick-tock-tick-tock, leaning against a closed door, watching the newspaper-reader sigh and refold his pages, the mother rummage in her bag for something to keep the toddler quiet, the tiny Oriental woman close her eyes and lapse into delicate snoring. All the while, Sonny not collecting a dime.

Taken as a whole, though, it wasn't bad work, with changing scenery and new folks along with the familiar faces. Those who spent most of their time aboveground didn't realize how two-dimensional their world was. Besides, he didn't have to serve people, and he didn't have to answer to a boss. He hadn't managed too well at any job with either of those requirements.

Sonny glanced out the subway window at the graffiti rushing past: illegible names, indecipherable drawings, puffy superhero writing.

Warnings, all, from another world. It was still too early to clock in—practically no customers yet. He could make use of the premature wake-up call to go to his sister's and take a shower, try to wash off his apprehensions along with the street dirt. It had been a week since his last shower, and staying clean was important in this job. A challenge, for sure, living and sleeping in rat territory, but if you started to smell bad, you got fewer handouts—or your salary dropped, as Sonny preferred to think of it. He'd seen it time and again, those poor suckers who allowed themselves to become rank on the way to becoming stupid. People shed liberal guilt, lost sympathy, turned away in disgust.

He liked his sister's place, a third-floor walk-up in the Bowery, on a little side street that was so far resisting the neighborhood's fix-up mood. Her husband, Leo, said they could afford better now and wanted to move, but Ruby was stuck on the area, and Sonny agreed. The Bowery was the city at its best—excepting, of course, for the subway. High-rise condos were on the way, no denying, but so far the fancy shops hadn't crowded everything out. Poor people weren't an extinct species yet. Still room for the occasional flophouse, under thirty bucks for a night, and where else on the island could you find that? 'Round the corner from Ruby's, the Bowery Mission folks served up inspirational hymns and three meals a day, just like they had since the 1800s. Squeezed between a tattoo parlor and a restaurant-supply store sat Steve's, a slop joint offering a cuppa for just a buck. If Sonny came in when the pot was near empty, they gave him the dregs for free, sometimes even throwing in a fresh roll. The people who spent four dollars for their coffee and needed choices of flavors and asked for soy milk instead of cream—those folks were farther uptown. In the Bowery, an outsider still felt at home. A bum could find a bed. And a passerby could still inhale the sweet scent of weed, come most nights. *Bhang*, an old Rasta had taught Sonny to call it, and though Sonny didn't smoke himself, he did enjoy catching a whiff as he passed. The scent of freedom.

The only problem with his sister's place was Leo. Leo felt ashamed to be related to someone in Sonny's line of business and couldn't keep that to himself. Sonny preferred to visit when Leo was out showing a client some overpriced condo or a fixer-upper, trying to persuade them that New York real estate wasn't priced for kings or working some new math to convince them they could spend more than they could afford. That meant daylight hours, when an apartment or a townhouse would be showing well, the sunlight spilling in, and Leo could pretend there were no shadows at all, folks desperate to believe that, anyway. Timing his visits to avoid Leo meant a shower usually cut into Sonny's own workday and wages, but what could you do?

Sundays were generally plenty busy for Leo, but it was too early still for clients to be house hunting. So maybe Sonny would ride instead to Coney Island, where the F train poked its nose aboveground after Church Street and he could peer down into a passing cemetery and turn philosophical if he wanted, or just catch himself some daylight from the comfort of the subway car. Maybe he'd head uptown to Columbus Circle, breathe in the perfumed women, and try to snag a left-behind newspaper so he could catch up on world events, some crisis in China or London that was moving across the world at light speed and might be just the thing that was affecting the mood today in Sonny's underground home office at what he considered the center of the earth.

One thing for sure: even if the mood belowground seemed as sour as meat gone bad, he didn't want to go above to walk aimless streets. It was too cold, the kind of acid wind-cold that bypassed your clothes and gnawed at your bones. The kind that brought a bitterness with it, as if it were taunting you about what might have been but wasn't, what could have happened but didn't. When you should have touched this or smelled that and you just let it slide on by, like you had forever.

You didn't have forever. You wanted to believe

the food would always taste good and the body keep on working fine enough and the trains always run, more or less on time. You wanted to believe there was no danger you couldn't scuttle from, and there never would be. That you'd always have another chance to set things right, figure it out, concentrate hard, kiss someone soft on the hollow at the base of her long neck, beg her to stay. But it wasn't true. One thing Sonny Hirt had been around long enough to learn: *forever* was a nasty lie, a red line across a neatly written page, a giggling kid with a needle in his arm. *Forever* was an opiate that blurred your vision and side-tracked you from doing what needed to be done. *Forever* was more deadening by far than the Bowery's *bhang*.

Vic arched her back, spun in a tight circle, and lifted her forehead as if to permit God to plant a kiss there. She felt the tip of her careless ponytail reach halfway down her back and was aware of the small beads of sweat that gathered in the tiny teardrop indentation above her lips. At a cue from the music, she spun around and sank to her knees, head lowered as if in prayer, then sprang up, extended again. *You are not human,* she told herself. *You are a flower, blooming, with the power to push away the earth itself.* With this vision in mind, she turned a leap into a glide. She heard Alex, watching from the third row of the theater on the Lower East Side, clap his hands. This was only rehearsal, but she made a brief, silent prayer to bring this same energy to the opening night.

Moving as sharply as she could, Vic shot forward from the waist and then reversed the motion, thrusting her pelvis to grind with another of the dancers—a redhead named Leslie, though Vic thought of her at this moment not as a woman but as pure form. She and Leslie twirled apart as a third dancer laughed on cue in a shrill way that still sounded eerie to Vic, even after all these rehearsals. The unnerving laughter was Alex's signature. She remembered him talking about what this choreography meant to him—"It's about how we cross boundaries for love. How we torture ourselves, we're desperate with longing, but we're all essentially and finally alone, forced to define personal integrity individually and, and—" Here he threw up his hands in frustration over the impossibility of translating the dance's passion into mediocre words—"that's the impulse. That's all."

Alex was a genius. She was thrilled, at age twenty-three, to be part of his company, even if he wasn't as widely recognized yet as he should be.

"All right, kids," Alex called from above. "Something isn't quite right in that one spot right before the culmination. You know what I'm talking about, Glenn and Vic. You two almost *collide*." He slapped his hands together and said the last word with comic drama.

Glenn, the only male in the company, playfully brushed Victoria's arm. "We have to save our colliding for offstage, Vic, honey," he said, and she laughed as if it were amusing, and then he said, "But seriously, you want me to back up at more of an angle?" and she said, "Doesn't that put you to the wrong side of the audience?" and Alex said, "You two, block it out again, will you?" their voices falling over one another in the hollowness of the theater like drops of water splashing into a glass as Alex said to the air, shaking his head, "Can you believe we're still messing with these details, and we open Tuesday night?"

"How about if I go here?" Vic asked Glenn, sliding one direction, and Glenn, moving another, answered, "Sweetie, that is *so* going to work," and Alex said, "You are beautiful, people. Beautiful!"

After another few minutes of this cacophony of conversation, Alex clapped his hands. "I need to dash out and pick up another container of helium for the balloons," he said. "So you have fifteen minutes, kids, while the cat's away. Everyone sip on your bubblies and breathe, breathe from the stomach, and then, my gems, we're going to run through it a few hundred more times."

Leslie, the redhead, groaned. "You're such a perfectionist, Alex. Who requires their dancers to come to practice at this hour of the morning? You, you, and only you."

"I get you fresh—" Alex began.

"And the work's the best," Leslie interrupted, using a singsong voice that made it clear this was Alex's typical line.

He just laughed. "If you get everything absolutely right when I'm back, we'll do it just twice more, so how's that for compromising? In that case, you'll be out of here by 10. But it's got to be right because I heard through the ubiquitous grapevine that the *Times* is sending someone opening night, giving us poor second-classers a chance at a life-altering review." He turned and, with a wave over his shoulder, bounced up the stairs. He was a bit heavier than any of the dancers

34

could afford to be, but he still moved with admirable agility.

Vic leaned over to rub her calves and then went to get her water bottle out of her bag. Leslie might complain, but she didn't mean it—they were all slaves to Alex's vision. Vic loved him for many things. But one thing she didn't love him for, she thought as she took a long sip from the bottle, was that she'd been so busy she hadn't had time to see, or even speak with, Jonas in a week. Maybe more. She'd tried to call a few times and hadn't gotten through. She was starting to ache for the guy. She pulled her cell phone from her bag and headed to the one section of the theater that seemed to get decent reception.

"Where you going, girl? Another phone call?" asked Glenn. She waved her hand at him.

The phone rang oddly for a moment and then went to voice mail: "It's Jonas. You know what to do." Should she leave another message? Would she start to seem pathetic? That was one thing she'd never been. She stared at the phone, then hung up. It was early; he was probably still asleep. She needed to stop by her mom's after rehearsal— she had to see how Mara was holding up. After that it would be late enough even for Mr. Sleepyhead. So after that, she'd call Jonas, and keep calling Jonas until she roused and reached him.

Carol leaned over the sink and splashed water on her face. She peered at herself in the mirror and dabbed some cream under her eyes. Funny, the way time had played with her; sometimes she looked good, maybe ten years younger than she actually was, and other times she looked at least ten years older. Now, although she felt edgy, nervous, and a little sick, she looked okay. There had been seasons, many, during Jonas's boyhood when she'd barely noticed her appearance. With Jonas gone—Jonas *out of the house,* she corrected herself—she'd begun paying a bit more attention. It seemed to matter more, though she couldn't say precisely why. She wasn't interested in adding anyone to her life, Lorenzo included.

What she wanted was to give more time to her work. She'd become involved lately in ceramic forms that were art first and vessels second. That took a certain confidence, to put form over function and think it would sell. She was exploring the juxtaposition of female curves with male lines within the architecture of a vase or a set of cups. Female curves, actually, arching away from male lines. A couple friends carried some of her work prominently in Manhattan galleries, and recently a gallery owner in Atlanta had e-mailed, offering to carry six or eight of her pieces. If she focused, she might be able to pull together a show somewhere. She'd been planning a full day of work, but it was more important today to make sure everything was solid with Jonas.

She went to the closet and pulled out an oversized sweater. Next to the closet hung five pictures of her son, one beneath the other, all of which she'd taken. The top photo showed Jonas at age three, vacuuming, an intent look in his eyes. Then Jonas at four and a half, dressed in a red firefighter's helmet. Jonas as a clown for Halloween, age ten, and Jonas, thirteen, sitting across the table from her in a restaurant—though she wasn't in the photo. She remembered the meal, his telling her he finally appreciated avocado, though the expression on his face as he ate a bite belied the claim. The bottom picture was Jonas, just turned seventeen, the high school graduate in cap and gown.

She'd been the right kind of mother for a boy— damnit, she *had*. Now she wanted to be the right kind of mother for a young man who felt things so deeply he didn't know how to process those feelings, where to put them. She still wanted to protect him—from others, from himself—and at the same time give him the space that would allow him to be honest with her, always. She was certainly flawed, but she was trying. She even wanted, eventually, to be the right kind of mother-in-law, though admittedly she wasn't sure such a thing was possible. She wasn't by nature anxiety-plagued. She hadn't been like this, in fact, when he'd been traveling out of the country; as long as he called a couple times a month, she felt fine. It was all out of her control, anyway.

Now, though, it felt like there *was* something she could do, even something she *should* do. Her son needed a mother now, or someone who cared as much as a mother—though why, what for? She had no idea. Her eyes tracked back to the photograph of him in the firefighter's hat, courtesy of the firehouse they'd visited in the Turtle Bay neighborhood not far from the United Nations. Jonas still had that round, glowing face of a pre-schooler. His eyes shone, probably with the excitement of the visit. He was smiling, too, but it was a serious smile, as if he already felt responsible for something. She reached out to touch his tiny image. "Hey, kid," she said, "you don't have to take it all on alone." Then, by the light of day half-believing and half-doubting her own intuition, she shook her head and made for the front door, grabbing her coat as she left.

NEW YORK: 10:47 A.M.
MECCA: 6:47 P.M.

Mara, listening outside the door. Ear pressed to it like a nosy parent checking a teenager's room, except that Mara was eleven, and she was listening to her mom. Stifled, intense soundlessness emanated from the other side of the door, and Mara knew what created that.

Mara, listening to her mother weeping. It qualified as weeping because it was thicker, fuller, and more private than mere crying. Her mother tried to hide the noise, to trap it in her throat. And so Mara thought of the weeping as an object with physical form that clogged her mother's windpipe, cutting off normal breath. Mara heard the repeated silence of her mother not breathing and then the sound of little gasping breaths. Mara feared her mother might eventually stop breathing altogether. That was one reason she listened—so that if the weeping halted and actual silence fell in its place, she could pound on the door. She imagined that she might even be able to break open the door— she'd heard of small people finding astonishing powers in extraordinary situations.

Mara listened, too, because she wanted to know certain things. She needed to know them, actually, here alone with her mother, and she didn't know how to find out. Asking wouldn't work because her mother wouldn't answer. So she listened hard, as if the weeping might tell her. She wanted to know, primarily, how long this might go on and how it would end. Sometimes she tried to think it through as if it were a scientific experiment. Take, as the first ingredient, a mother who rarely goes to work as she used to because the office that used to belong to her and Daddy is somehow only Daddy's office now, and who rarely goes to the grocery store as if that were too challenging, and who rarely bathes or brushes her hair, and who emerges from her room for no more than three hours a day. Combine that with a disconnected voice on the phone, at once authoritative and tentative, who is the father, living, apparently cheerfully, someplace without the mother. Then add a daughter who spends her Saturday hovering outside a bedroom door in an apartment eight floors above the city, listening to the mother weep. What was the end product? Mara had no immediate hypothesis. She had to take it step by step. Materials, procedures, observations. And then conclusion. Mara was good in science, very good, though her grades had recently begun to drop. For the moment, Mara was balancing homework with Mom-alert.

If Vic still lived at home instead of in her own place downtown, or if she even had more time between dance rehearsals, maybe Mara wouldn't feel so responsible, so involved in her mother's tears. There'd be two daughters to share in this. And of course, if her dad still lived here, Mara wouldn't be responsible at all. The weeping had begun about six weeks ago and her dad had left a month ago and at that point the weeping had gotten worse. Her father and Vic had to know what was happening with Mara's mother. But everyone in her family always called Mara "the little angel," so maybe they thought she spread her wings and floated to some serene place while her mother cried. Maybe they thought Mara didn't need help.

Since it was all up to her, Mara had been working to fine-tune her aural senses. That way she could better hear the sounds that had become primary in her life: doors opening and closing, and her mother's muted tears. Mara's method: she filled the bathtub just enough to cover her ears and then lay down. Listening through water made the unnecessary sounds go away—the cars passing on the street below, or an airplane overhead. Miraculously, it also magnified the small, necessary ones, the internal sounds. All she had to do was pay attention, and she could make out the hisses of the old couple next door arguing in Russian. She could hear the rumble of the subway that ran directly beneath their building and even, she believed, the voices of commuters talking. She could hear the walls breathe. She would lie there until her skin grew dimpled from moisture and the water began to cool and goose bumps rose on her body. Later she could hear from the other end of the apartment when her mother finally cracked open her bedroom door and quietly emerged, almost shamefacedly, as if she were tip-toeing in after curfew. Then Mara could run to join her for as long as she stayed outside the cave of her bedroom, as long as she could hold the tears at bay. Even when the door remained closed and Mara had to press herself against it for comfort, the listening exercise paid off. Sometimes, it was true, Mara couldn't hear anything except sirens and traffic helicopters. But in general, the under-tone of weeping appeared to grow louder and clearer as Mara's hearing sharpened.

Today Mara's mother had been shuttered in her room for the past four hours. With luck, she would come out of the bedroom, blinking as if she'd emerged from darkness, and say, "How about some scrambled eggs?" though it was way past breakfast time. Or she'd ask some question about school, though it was Sunday. Or she'd squeeze Mara's shoulders and suggest an activity, though they wouldn't end up actually doing it. She would smile and be cheerful, especially if the phone rang, and Mara would be grateful, but she would not be fooled. It would be a case of barely hanging on, like when Mara had to do chin-ups during gym, and before long her mother would scuttle back into the bedroom and the door would close.

She'd once overheard her dad's racquetball partner say kids knew everything. The partner—a tall, mostly bald psychologist—often made silly pronouncements, but in this case she knew he was right. At least, partially right. Kids knew everything about their families—maybe because their families *were* everything for a while, the entire world squeezed into a few people and a small space. Kids had nothing else to pay attention to, so they soaked it all up. But one point the psychologist failed to make: knowing something was a long way from understanding it.

This latest weepisode, as Mara privately called them, had been touched off by a morning phone call from Mara's father that had come as her mother was in the kitchen, putting on water to boil. Her mother gaily answered the phone and then slipped into the bedroom, pulling the door behind her slowly so it closed with a quiet but definite click, and her voice grew too low to catch, and Mara turned off the stove and then debated with herself for about two minutes before she went into the bathroom near the kitchen. An old-fashioned black candlestick phone stood on a small hand-painted table, a whimsical decorative item chosen during more cheerful times. It was the best phone, and the best location, for telephone eavesdropping. She lifted it up carefully, as she'd learned from Vic. Noiselessly, midconversation.

"Down the street, there's this pool hall. Back

Door Billiards." Mara's father's voice nearly trembled with warmth and intimacy. "A restaurant at the corner sells Jamaican patties, hot and spicy."

"For God's sake," Mara's mother said, almost under her breath.

"It's all so real, Lynne. Everything else in my life had stopped being authentic."

"Everything?"

Mara's father sighed. "I'm not trying to *hurt* you. I'm trying to *explain*."

"Shit," she said.

"I'm forty-seven," he said. "I have to look at this." For a moment, all Mara heard was her mother strangling on her breath, and then her father spoke again. "There's this saying around here: *De higher de monkey climb, de more he expose.* I've been thinking about that. Maybe I just, I saw too many monkeys climbing too high. It seems pointless now."

"I don't know what you're talking about," Mara's mother said, and Mara could hear in her voice that she was wrestling with an enormous force, still winning for the moment, still calm or calm enough, but not yet the final victor. "Moving from the Upper West Side, five minutes from the office, into a small, dingy flat an hour and twenty minutes away in Brooklyn doesn't give your life more meaning."

"But that's what I'm trying to say, Lynne.

You're not listening. The work, the apartment, our little neighborhood—for quite some time now, it's all felt artificial."

"Don," she said, and Mara could hear that she was straining her patience to its limit, "Jamaican patties and Sunday gospels isn't *your* reality. It's not authentic to *you*."

"Why couldn't it be?"

"No. Stop." Mara's mother's voice sounded like broken glass, and Mara could almost see her waving her arms. "Oh. God. Just stop." The line was silent for a beat, and then she spoke again, and it was clear she'd begun to cry. "You think I don't *know* this? How stupid do you think I am? This isn't about goddamn *authenticity*. This is a lot more cliché even than that. This is about you banging that," she caught her breath, "that Caribbean author Vic's age—"

Mara yanked the phone away from her ear, not sure what her father meant by "authentic" or the monkeys thing but certain that she was finished listening. She quietly replaced the receiver.

Since then, lingering outside her mother's door, she'd been thinking about how to change things for her mother—would a kitten help? Should she throw a party? Maybe buy some cupcakes at the bakery on 81st? It all seemed a bit lame. She was wishing a solution would just pop into her head, the way answers sometimes did on multiple-choice tests, when she heard a key in the door. She wondered, for a breath, if it might be her father, fresh from Brooklyn and here to talk things through with her mother. Sometimes, as her father said, her mother didn't really listen; she seemed so lost in her own thoughts—always had, now that Mara considered it. Maybe a good set of ears from his wife was all her father needed, and he'd returned to claim it.

But of course it was not her father at the door. Her father would not simply wander back in at this point. There would be no magic wand; this was not a musical. Mara herself was going to have to figure out how to fix it.

She moved away from her mother's bedroom door, still shuttered, and headed toward the living room. "Hey, Vic," she called out, because only one other person had keys to their apartment.

"Mar-muffin, the angel." Vic stood smiling in the center of the room, holding a white plastic bag with one hand, her hair pulled away from her face. Vic was so beautiful she glowed, literally, as though her skin were a thin veneer covering pure gold. Mara was smart, really smart; she knew that. She'd been tested, and though her parents didn't discuss it because they thought it unhealthy to dwell on, she knew the scores had surprised even them. But she also had wiry, brittle hair and a small, sharp nose. She wore glasses. She had bony shoulders that gave her prominent angel wings, contributing to the family nickname. As to which would prove in the end more useful, being smart enough and very beautiful or very smart and not too attractive, she hadn't yet figured out.

"I'm so sorry. It's been insanely busy. Rehearsals—well, you know. I've missed you, though, baby. I brought a loaf of whole-grain and some sawbies," Vic said, using the word Mara used to say when she was a toddler, before she could say "strawberries."

"We already have sawbies," said Mara, flinging one arm behind her toward her parents'—her mother's—bedroom, with a play on the words she knew her sister would get.

"Jeez," Vic said. And then, "Mom?" And in a louder, more authoritative tone, "Mom."

After a long moment, the bedroom door pushed open, the hinges squeaking a little in protest, making Mara think of muscles stiff from disuse. Her mother swept in, arms open. She wore jeans and a fresh, long-sleeved white shirt. Her tangled hair, blond with a few scattered strands of silver, fell to just below her shoulders; her face was splotchy and mirror-shiny at once. "Vic!" she said almost manic-gaily, adding, "Mara!" a moment later, as though Mara had just arrived as well. She pulled both daughters into her arms, rocking them for a moment, and then said in a bright tone, "What time is it, girls? Shall we have some breakfast?"

"Breakfast?" Vic glanced at Mara. "What'd you eat today?"

Mara didn't respond. Vic didn't know how bad it had gotten.

Vic shook her head. "C'mon," she said. "Let's wash the berries."

Their mom followed them into the kitchen—as if she were the kid, Mara thought—and sat, crossing her arms on top of the table. Vic pulled a brush from her purse and handed it to Mara. "You brush," she said, gesturing toward their mother's head. "I'll do food."

Mara took the brush and pulled out some of Vic's golden auburn hair, twirling it around her finger and setting it carefully on the table. Then she held the brush over her mother's scalp for a second. Mara was uncoordinated; that was another thing about her. While Vic was a dancer who seemed to control her body as easily as she might lift a cup to her lips, Mara had trouble cutting along a straight line for school projects. Sometimes she wondered how she and Vic could be sisters. She lowered the brush and began slowly working on her mother's hair. Her mother allowed it, even leaned her head back a little, her eyes narrowing as she watched Vic at the sink.

"Have you gotten thinner over the last couple weeks?" their mother asked.

Vic shrugged. "Same as always, I think," she said over her shoulder. "Though Alex has been working us." She bent to a lower cabinet to find a colander.

"Hmm." Her mother tapped her fingers on the table. "Are you . . ." she paused, ". . . seeing anyone?"

Mara stared at Vic, eager to hear how Vic would answer. She liked catching little bits of a world removed, one in which she didn't yet have to participate. She was also curious because Mara knew something that her mother, caught up in her own drama, had failed to notice. Mara knew—at least she was pretty sure—that Vic liked Jonas. At another time, a pre-Dad-leaving time, this would have been big news. Vic and Jonas had been friends since high school, when he lived four blocks away and they used to share meals at each other's houses, do homework together. Jonas had even seen Vic with pimple cream on her nose. No big deal.

About three weeks ago, though, Vic came to visit and brought Jonas with her, and Mara saw that something had changed. When Mara walked into the living room, they were standing near the window, their fingers barely touching, and they were looking at each other in a certain way that startled Mara, then scared her for a second, and then made her feel like giggling—from embarrassment, mainly. But she was glad. Jonas was sweet. Jonas was the only one who seemed to notice Mara—at one point during the visit, he knelt down to Mara and asked, "How's it going?" and when she shrugged, he squeezed her shoulder and said, "It will get better. Promise." Mara thought if she had a brother, she wouldn't mind him being like Jonas.

Vic waved her right hand in the air dismissively. "Dancing is taking up all my time right now."

"Well," said their mother, and then she stopped, but she looked pleased. "How are rehearsals coming?"

"Good." Vic brightened. "Want to come opening night? It's Tuesday, remember."

"Is your father . . . ?"

Vic sighed audibly. "No, Mom." She turned on the kitchen faucet and began rinsing the strawberries.

"Just—just asking," their mother said. Then she closed her eyes and leaned her head back a little into Mara's brushing. She seemed to relax, and that allowed Mara to relax, too. Mara thought about the sense of peace that came from listening to Vic busy herself at the kitchen sink, and she thought about what it would be like to be grown-up and to be the one who brought that comfort to someone else. She tried to imagine herself Vic's age, but it seemed too far away to envision. When she was very little, five or six, after a family road trip to California, Mara told her parents she'd decided to grow up to be a billboard painter and paint new billboards every day that would make drivers feel peaceful instead of wanting to honk their horns. She was too young to understand her parents' amused reaction. A few years later, she announced she would write a book that her parents would edit, though what kind of book remained uncertain since her mother worked on nonfiction and her father edited poetry. A poetic book about pretzel baking, or maybe mountain climbing? That plan, too, drew indulgent smiles. Now, when she closed her eyes and thought about the future, it seemed fuzzy, full of sharp edges and dark holes and no colors at all. Was this only since her father had left? She couldn't remember.

Vic turned off the faucet as their mother murmured.

"What?" Vic turned.

"Oh. Oh, nothing. He just takes himself too seriously, your father." She cleared her throat. "Do you see him much?" Her voice was affected. She was trying to pretend the question was casual.

"Mom," said Vic, "I don't want to talk about Dad, or you and Dad. If I get involved, I'm going to end up having to pay two hundred bucks a week for three years of therapy. As a dancer, I can't afford it."

Their mother waved her hand, her eyes still closed. The gesture was unclear: Did she accept Vic's refusal, or was she waiting for a chance to ask again? Vic seemed concentrated on cutting the ends off the strawberries, and for a few minutes the only sound was the brush pulling through their mother's hair.

"Don't hold close to anything, girls," their mother said at last. "That's my best piece of maternal advice. Don't count on anything because everything changes and that's *all* you can count on."

Mara looked up from her mother's hair to exchange a glance with Vic. When their mom began talking to them like that, making pronouncements and saying "girls," it meant nothing good. It meant she was feeling morose. That had been true even before their dad had moved out.

"Isn't that kind of a cliché, Mom?" Mara said, not unkindly. In fact, she sounded like her mother herself, who used to point out clichés when looking over Vic's or Mara's school papers. Their mother ignored her.

"Some changes are for the best. Sure, they are," their mother said. "Learning how to make rice pudding. Consummating my relationship with your father. Earning more money. Those were *good* changes."

Vic grabbed a dishtowel, held it under the colander, and brought the strawberries to the table. "Eat," she said to Mara.

"But the rest—well, the bottom line is, cling to nothing. Even when I was your age, Vic, and I could feel men watching me as I walked down the street, and even when my energy was boosted by every breath I took, I knew what was coming.

That eventually my hair would lose its sheen, my skin would turn fragile, and I wouldn't bounce up a set of stairs."

"Mom," Vic said, "you look great. Besides, *everything* doesn't change."

"What? What doesn't change?" Their mother's voice had grown loud and a bit harsh, the way she had spoken to their father at the end, in the days before he'd left.

"Mom," Vic said soothingly, "we're always going to be your daughters."

Her mother shook her head as though to shrug Mara off, so Mara stopped brushing. "No more cribs, no more wet wipes or playgrounds. You live in your own apartment, and Mara will be next," their mother said, not pausing to allow Mara to protest that she wasn't yet in high school. "It changes. It already has. So. Name one thing that doesn't."

Vic shook her head and looked up at the ceiling. "Memories," she said after a minute, grinning like she'd called out the right answer on a game show. "Memories don't change."

"Are you kidding?" their mother said. "Whatever happens in the future makes whatever happened in the past look different. Sometimes completely different. Try again."

Vic sat at the table and leaned forward. She hesitated, her expression searching and determined. Mara was rooting for her older sister, although in much the way one would root for an underdog —full of doubt and trepidation. And then Vic smiled. "The stones."

The stones. Yes. Vic was brilliant to remember them. Everywhere they went over the years, the four of them collected everything from large pebbles to small rocks and brought them home. The stones were rich with memories—their own family memories and those that predated them, their mother said. The stones were their family's version of a photo album. Sometimes for special meals, they put four or five in a pile on the table, a centerpiece. Generally they were kept in two bowls on the bookcase. Vic and Mara had spent many hours sorting through them. Their dad sometimes carried one in his pocket, and after a hard day, their mother would sit in a chair by the window and rub one.

Their mother stared at the palm of her right hand as though she could see her future there. "Even stones change," she said. "Smoothed by waves. Pitted by sand." But her voice sounded less certain. "And wind . . ." She trailed off.

"Those stones are exactly the same as the first time we brought them into the house, Mom." Vic handed Mara another strawberry before she moved to the living room and then returned, bringing a bowl of stones with her.

Mara's mother glanced at them, then turned her face to the wall.

"Look at the quartz streaks in this one," Vic said, holding one out and waiting until their mom took it. "Remember how we found it on that trip to the Southwest?"

"And this orange one with a smooth spot in the middle of all the rough," Mara said, emboldened by Vic's success. "Remember how Vic used to say it was the stone with a stomach?"

"And this one, Mara, you said looked like a peach with a bite missing," said Vic.

Their mother looked at both of them. "You girls," she said, and finally, shaking her head, she laughed. She actually laughed. It sounded gentle, like a real laugh, and it filled Mara with hope, and with a sharp longing she'd been denying—a yearning for those old days when twice as many people lived in this apartment, and it felt alive, and she'd never felt scared, like she did sometimes now, of shadows that stood in corners.

Their mother reached for the bowl, letting her fingers skim over several stones before she selected one. "This is the one that fits in your eye," she said to Vic. "Remember?"

"And this one," said Vic, "I used to be able to balance it on the bridge of my nose." She tried, but it fell to the table and all three of them laughed. Mara loved the way laughter made her chest feel lighter. She'd never noticed that before, in the old days. Still laughing, she reached up and pulled another stone out of the bowl.

"Look at this one," she said, giggling. "The lopsided heart."

As soon as she said it, she knew she'd made a mistake. Her father had collected the heart stone along a Scottish beach where her parents had spent a week alone together when she'd been a toddler. She still vaguely remembered staying with Vic at their grandmother's house in Virginia. Her father had hidden the stone in his luggage until Valentine's Day, and then, sitting at this very table, he'd given it to their mother and recited some silly rhyming poem he'd written himself on the 1-train on the way home from work the night before. Mara didn't remember actually witnessing that part, but she'd been told over the years. A favorite Valentine's Day memory.

Their mother looked at Mara, her gaze accusing, and then got up.

"Mom?" Vic said.

"Be right back," their mother said, her voice sounding labored. They heard the bedroom door close. Vic looked at Mara.

"She won't be right back," Mara said quietly.

"How long will she stay in there?" Vic asked.

Mara shrugged, feeling loyalty toward her mother surge up from somewhere unexpected. She wondered how much she should reveal. "A long time," she said noncommittally, hoping Vic could read between those words.

"Well, I guess it's better than screaming," Vic

said. "With Jonas's parents, there was screaming."

Mara would have preferred screaming to the apartment's eerie, constant silence, but she didn't say that. "How is Jonas?" Mara asked. It was an adult-sounding question, a question their mother or father might have asked at a different time.

Vic smiled. "Fine." She ruffled Mara's hair. Then she picked up a strawberry from the colander and rotated it between her fingers. "I'm going to make you a sandwich," she said. "Do we have cheese?" She put down the strawberry, opened the refrigerator, and began moving food around, scrounging.

"Vic, I'm sorry," Mara said after a minute.

"For what?" Vic pulled some Dijon mustard from the refrigerator door.

"You know. Saying that about the heart stone." Her carelessness made her feel so guilty that her stomach actually hurt, and she rubbed it gently.

"Oh, angel." Vic paused to give her a hug. "Mom's got to stop being so damn sensitive. Maybe she needs to take antidepressants."

"She won't do that. You remember that book she edited about overmedicated America."

Vic sliced some cheese, placed it on the bread, and added lettuce. She set the sandwich before Mara. "Eat," she said.

Mara took a big bite. The cheese was a little dry and the bread a bit stale, but she didn't mind much. Vic brought her a big glass of orange juice, and she drank some of that, too. "You know, Vic," she said after a minute, "I have an idea about what we can do."

"What do you mean?"

"How we're going to make Dad come back."

Vic sat down, her slender form suddenly seeming heavy. "Sweetie," she began, but Mara decided to ignore her.

"If Dad knew how sad Mom really was—" Mara began.

"I think he knows, sweetie."

Mara shook her head. "Every time he calls, you should hear her—she sounds really happy, like she's just gotten home from a party or something. And then they start fighting. So he probably thinks she's doing fine *until* he calls. But, Vic, she's like some zombie." That was the most explicit Mara had ever permitted herself to be to anyone about her mother over this past month.

Vic stood up, moved behind Mara, and began massaging her shoulders. "They're so tight," she said, but Mara shrugged her off. She didn't want to be pacified, not now.

"You know how softhearted Dad is," Mara said. "Whenever we got hurt, remember? Mom told us to buck up, but Dad came running with the bandages and the worried expression. He wouldn't want Mom to feel this way. So we'll take him the stones, get him remembering, and then we'll tell him how bad it is, how much she misses him."

Vic sighed. "Look, sweetie—"

"He loves these stones. He used to say they held magic, remember?"

"But you heard Mom. Memories *do* change."

"We can't take them all on the subway, but we don't need all. Just this one," Mara lifted a black-and-white speckled rock, "and this," choosing the one that looked like the partly eaten peach, "and this," picking up the lopsided heart, cradling it in the palm of her hand.

"Baby, I think it's more complicated than that."

Mara *knew* it was complicated; of course she knew that. She thought about mentioning their mother's reference to a Caribbean author to prove it. "There's always a way to simplify," Mara said. "Like the answer to a math problem. Right down to the prime numbers."

Vic smiled. She took Mara's hand, and this time Mara let her. "I'm sorry. I know this is hard for you, still being at home." Vic shook her head and added, almost as an aside, "Why couldn't he wait, damnit?"

"Mom can't go on like this," Mara said. She wanted to add, "I can't," but she didn't.

Vic rose and released a deep, sighing breath. "So talk to Dad if you want. Just don't blame yourself if it doesn't work, okay?"

"But I thought—" Mara stopped. What she'd thought was that Vic would help her; she'd counted on it, assumed it didn't even need to be said. She wouldn't act like a baby about it, though. Lots of things she used to depend on were changing, and maybe that was what it meant to grow up.

"You okay, angel?" Vic said.

"Hmm." Mara nodded.

Vic lifted one foot, grabbed her ankle behind her back, and stretched out her leg. "Already getting stiff," she said, laughing softly. "It was one long rehearsal. I'm going home to take a shower and a rest. I'll call, okay?"

So, fine. Mara would do it alone. She could go tomorrow morning. She'd take the subway to Brooklyn early so she could be there before her dad went to work. If all went well, maybe he would drive her home and they could go into the apartment together. Her mom wouldn't be happy that Mara had cut school, but she'd understand once it was all explained.

"Hey, you in the fog. Plotting away, are you? Give me a hug good-bye, okay?" Vic pulled her close and bent so their heads were touching. "It'll be all right," she murmured.

"I know." Mara straightened, feeling the responsibility that came with seeing what had to be done. Vic was like their mom, wanting everyone to buck up, so Mara would have to be like their dad, bearing the Band-Aids. "I know."

Vic pulled away and ruffled her hair again. Mara hated the gesture for its implied meaning. But they would know, soon enough, that she was not a kid. She followed her sister into the living room and watched as Vic, with one last wave, closed the door firmly behind her, leaving Mara and her mother inside.

Jonas supposed he was meant to just keep praying, pray all day as if he were in Mecca on the hajj, dip his forehead to the ground and pray to the hurricane-god of subways roaring, sirens wailing, whores and stockbrokers shouting numbers, matrons grasping, vacationers exclaiming in a mix of tongues, this animal of a city issuing its collective hungry growl, but he had wearied, finally, of the mixed CD of prayers Masoud had burned for him, and he was finding it hard to come up with a prayer—a fresh prayer that would mean something—on an empty stomach. He should have brought groceries for the kitchenette, but no one had mentioned it in the list of directives, so he'd brought only tea bags and bottled water. Anyway, he'd thought food wouldn't interest him, since it hadn't much for weeks. But he'd been wrong. He wanted, almost desperately, something warm in his mouth. Something fiery-spicy that would titillate as it satisfied. Tomorrow Jonas's day belonged to a greater cause. Tomorrow he would be pure energy, a spark and a flash, a name on a million lips. But today he was still just Jonas, Manhattan Jonas, Upper West Side Jonas, young man Jonas, with a young man's appetite, with dreams, in fact, of a hot sandwich made from lamb. Today Jonas wanted a gyro.

After the last 120 hours of intensive training during which Jonas had slept very little and hadn't been able to slip away even to call Vic, Masoud had dropped him off at this apartment with strict instructions that he should have no further contact with anyone. Masoud didn't elaborate, and Jonas decided now that he would interpret that to mean no one he knew. Mothers and girlfriends might be one thing, but surely Masoud hadn't meant to rule out contact with average people on the street, people who wouldn't remember him if they saw him again fifteen minutes later. He needed more razors to finish the shaving job, and besides that, if he went out, if he stayed in, who would know? He was in a void, a space intended to allow deeper connection to Allah. The only human visitor he expected was Masoud, and that wouldn't be until this evening.

He went into the kitchen, opened the refrigerator, and took a photograph of his own hand reaching into its emptiness. He was already sick of this ground-floor studio apartment with its anorexic bed, its yawning gray walls, its floor naked save for the prayer rug Masoud had placed in a corner. It seemed that once he was gone, they wanted nothing to show he'd ever been here. The result, though, was that nothing proved he was here right now. That felt like an erasure come too soon.

He wondered what Deirdre had done the day

before she'd driven that bomb-laden car to Armagh, in Ireland. He imagined her calm, focused, sleeping normally, her wavy auburn hair fanned out over her pillow. He doubted she'd needed rituals to calm her; she'd had a boyfriend nearly a decade older than she who, she told Jonas, had simply been using her. She could live with being used, though, she said, because she believed what she did at the tail end of the Troubles helped to resolve them. She believed in the rightness of her actions. He'd been crazy about her—her sexual appetite, her milky skin and green eyes, her grasp of European history, even the ways in which she was messy, with piles of dirty clothes next to plates of half-eaten food. But he knew now he must have seemed like a child to her. He was nineteen; she was thirty-one. He was briefly exotic to her—this intense blond traveling boy from America who found himself in Belfast—and then she wearied of him.

But when she heard about this, she'd think more of him. She might even admire him.

He tugged up his jeans—he'd lost twelve pounds in the last three weeks—and pulled on his water-resistant, down-filled parka. Before leaving, he held the camera away from his face and took another picture, this one of his head and shoulders reflected in the bathroom mirror. In his mind, he titled the photograph *Jonas, hungry for gyro.*

Outside the tall red-brick building of stacked apartments, the wind ignored his high-technology parka and went right for the bone. This was serious cold. In most towns, the streets would be bare on such a day, but no one who lived in New York City could afford to take time off and stay cozy inside, and nothing deterred the endless tourists in their frenzied, thoughtless race from museum to restaurant to theater. So the streets were still full enough, though each face was etched with a matching grimace and each body charged forward as if lingering could kill.

Jonas headed toward the tip of Manhattan, where the East River mates with the Hudson. His ungloved fingers quickly began to sting from the cold, but he only had to walk two and a half blocks before he found a deli, windows slightly steamed. Three bells hanging from a rope clanged as he shoved open the door. The deli, squeezed into a railroad-car-sized space, carried a thick scent of coffee. Beyond a display crammed with single-serving bags of chips, Jonas saw meat spinning on a kebab over a grill. The man behind the counter wore a white apron with an oil stain on his left chest, near his heart. He nodded once at Jonas, the only customer.

"Hey," Jonas said.

The man watched him, impassive.

"A gyro," Jonas said. "Lamb. Extra white sauce and extra hot sauce."

"You got it, bud."

The man reached for the pita bread, and Jonas noticed he had dark, fur-like hair on his arms, almost matted to his skin. This guy would have a tough time doing what Jonas had just done, shaving much of his body; it would probably take him hours, and even then, he almost certainly had hair in places that he couldn't reach, places Jonas didn't want to consider.

"Carrotsonionstomatoes?" the man asked, as if they were one word.

Jonas nodded. "The works."

It occurred to Jonas that maybe Masoud had chosen him simply because he didn't have a mass of body hair, so no one would have to help him shave. He smiled at that thought. On the other hand, as much as Jonas wanted to believe his passion and intellectual clarity were what had singled him out, he knew the deciding factor was probably that he came from privilege. At least relative privilege, American-style. A home, a laptop, an iPod, plenty of food, clothes, education. And this, his comparative wealth, would increase the public impact of his deed. Its marketability, if you will. It gave his actions greater meaning. Masoud had explained this, and Jonas believed him. He understood that if people saw someone like him—like *them*—moved to carry out such a mission, to make such a sacrifice, then they would have to ask themselves why. They would have to question their assumptions because Jonas would not be so easy to dismiss. And the act of questioning would force people to realize how America's powerful triteness undermined not only the country but the world itself. The climax was coming. Jonas had been aware of this well before he'd met Masoud. For a long time, in fact, he'd found himself unable to ignore the flawed and increasingly frail pretend-wizard behind the curtain. Oz was a made-up place, and more and more of his countrymen were beginning to realize that. The momentum caused by his act—well, that was in the hands of something greater than Jonas, but he believed it could lead to a consequential awakening in America.

His ability to spot the wizard behind the curtain had for years plunged Jonas into periodic depressions. How did everyone else manage their lives without being brought to a halt by the government's lies, its narrow-mindedness, its violence against those who did not believe or adhere? Maybe he'd just been born with some gene—either one extra or one missing—that left him deformed for American life. Either way, the fact that he recognized the situation meant he had to do something. Something significant. The Gandhi alternative seemed grandiose and improbable in the current day. This was an age of sanctioned violence—air strikes, not hunger strikes. Deirdre had made that clear long before Jonas had met Masoud. And so, although Masoud had approached him, Jonas believed *he* had actually done the choosing. His personal search had led him to precisely this moment.

"Here you go, bud," the man said, handing over a sandwich wrapped in foil. Jonas didn't want to eat while walking the icy streets—difficult to manage and clearly a poor choice for his last New York gyro. Though this was not a sit-in deli, a table with one folding chair stood in the far corner.

"You mind?" Jonas asked, motioning toward the chair with his head. The man shrugged, and Jonas sat.

As he peeled back the foil from the stuffed pita, Jonas decided to bring a Buddhist approach to eating the gyro; he wanted to be fully present and taste each bite. He thought about Buddhist monks in Tibet who ate very little but chewed so slowly that a twelve-bite meal could take an hour. He'd learned this particular detail from a former monk he'd met in the comparative religion class at SAWU—the same place he'd initially met Masoud. Harold was a surprise—a middle-aged guy in jeans and a T-shirt with a hole in the right sleeve and a slogan reading, "Bud, King of Beers," who'd spent a year and a half as a novice monk, living in a monastery near Lhasa in a room the size of a walk-in closet, trying to make sense of things. That was the way he'd expressed it, without elaboration: "Trying to make sense of things." Then he'd decided to shove it in and come back home, where he'd ended up in a class with Jonas and they'd begun talking food.

"New Yorkers wolf down breakfast and lunch and only slow down for dinner half the time. There, living with the monks, I consciously tasted every bite." Harold scratched his head thoughtfully. "Made me appreciate the mouthful, sure. Problem was, I was also slowly starving." Jonas and Harold enjoyably split hairs, then, over the various ways of starving. Jonas said too much food could also lead to starvation, and Harold said, "Listen, you goddamn idealist, a man can't even recognize the metaphorical unless he's got a belly full enough," and their argument continued, good-naturedly and off-and-on, for a couple weeks.

Now Jonas grinned, thinking about telling Masoud, the pious Muslim who'd completed the hajj in Mecca, that he'd spent his last day trying to eat Buddhist-style. On second thought, Masoud would probably appreciate that—Masoud was not an extremist as Jonas had once thought of them—except that he was extremely well-educated. He'd studied topics that swept from the earth to the sky and had easy access to facts that seemed obscure to Jonas. In one of their early discussions, Masoud casually mentioned that Socrates was the Western world's first recorded martyr, ordered to die for insisting that all men and women possessed souls of their own and thus were obliged to question authority and discover truth for themselves. "The martyr is the offspring of a community at war with itself," Masoud said. "The martyr helps the right side win. And so beyond his death, he continues to live in two realms, Paradise and Earth."

Masoud was often open-minded as well; in fact, the main difference between Masoud and, say, Jonas's dad was that Masoud, having lost his older brother, had thought through the meaning and purpose of his life, and that consciousness guided his actions, whereas Jonas's dad's life, like most people's, had been shaped by chance and longing and failure. To the outside world, Masoud might look like a struggling grad student and Jonas's father like a thriving art dealer, but looks deceived.

The pita felt warm against Jonas's lips. He hesitated long enough to consciously absorb the heat and then bit down. Delicious—it was moist and spicy, and he imagined he could distinguish the individual flavors: tomatoes, and onions, and green peppers. And the lamb, the sacrificial lamb. He ate slowly, savoring each bite, feeling the carrots crunch and the tender lamb give way under his teeth, and after a few bites he tried to catch the eye of the man in the apron, wanting to nod his appreciation, but the man had lost interest in him; he was standing at the other end of the deli, gazing out the window at the street. Just then the bell hanging from the door rang again and two young women walked in, one wearing a black coat and the other a red jacket and mittens. The red-jacket woman had black hair, pale skin, and saucy full lips.

The man behind the counter grew suddenly more attentive. "Yes, ladies?"

"I'll take a hot pastrami on rye," the black coat said. "And a cup of coffee, to go."

"And you, miss?"

"Oh, I guess . . ." The red-jacket woman hesitated, reading the menu from a board above the man's head. "Swiss on a roll?"

"Sure thing," the man said.

"So anyway," the red-jacket woman turned to her friend, clearly picking up midconversation, "it was disgusting. He pressed himself up against me and—" She hesitated, glancing toward Jonas, then apparently decided to disregard him. "I could feel his dick against my back."

"Oh, God," the other woman said. "What did you do?"

"I waited a second until I was sure I wasn't imagining it, and then I said in a loud voice, 'Get the fuck away from me.' And he said, 'What are you talking about, lady? The subway is crowded. I can't get away from you.' He started talking to the other passengers: 'What is this lady, crazy? Doesn't she know this is rush hour?' God, he was an asshole." The woman looked at Jonas again and scowled while her friend murmured sympathetically. Jonas averted his gaze to his lap. After a moment, the woman resumed talking. "I said, 'Don't fuck with me; you're fuckin' feeling me up.'"

Jonas felt his cheeks flush with a sudden rush of fury. He felt incensed with the man who had harassed this woman on the subway, certainly. But he was also angry with the woman in the red jacket for expressing herself so crudely in a deli so tiny that he was forced to hear every word. He glanced over at the man making the sandwiches, and this time the man returned his gaze, winked, and nodded toward the women with a leering smile. The moment reeked of vulgarity—precisely the trait that was undermining this country and had to change.

We never destroyed a population that had not a term decreed and assigned beforehand. Neither can a people anticipate its Term, nor delay it. Sura 15: 4–5.

Jonas's appetite had vanished. He left the last piece of his gyro on the table and paused near the women, waiting until they looked at him before pushing his way out the door. *I want you to remember me,* he thought. *Remember when you see me on TV.*

The street seemed a bit warmer, whether because of the sandwich in his stomach or because of his anger. He felt suddenly aimless. These were the hours in between. Nearly all the time and for a long time now—for the last ten or twelve weeks of study, at least, and certainly during the final intensive training with Masoud—he'd had no chance to feel aimless. In fact, as the weeks had passed, he'd grown increasingly focused. He'd felt remarkably clear-headed since converting to Islam, a simple ceremony carried out in a small mosque with Masoud present several days before Jonas left for Pakistan. The conversion involved stating his intention in a ritual way and then washing to symbolically rinse away his previous life. Jonas recognized that he converted primarily out of a sense of brotherhood with Masoud, who'd lost his own birth-brother. But he did love certain things about Islam—the physical act of praying, for instance, bowing together, rising, a human wave of committed energy, an act of beauty on both the micro- and the macroscale. He liked the discipline of Islam's daily routine, and its intimacy, that there were few human intercessors between him and Allah. He very much liked that Islam offered him a path to finally make a difference, and how it seemed to anticipate his doubts, his crisis of confidence, and be ready with answers. When it came to religion, he was happy to pick and choose parts of each he encountered.

Over the last weeks, Jonas and Masoud had discussed religion and philosophy for hours each day. Masoud repeatedly described the Ka'ba in Mecca, always dense with prayer, and together they pondered what Mohammed's life must have been like there and what the world might be in ten years. They talked politics, too, and discussed the death of Masoud's brother Ifraan, and the vast numbers of others killed by American bombs and rockets. Masoud explained *qisas*, the Islamic law that requires equality in punishment, much like the biblical mandate to take an eye for an eye. Sometimes Masoud woke Jonas at 2 or 3 in the morning to offer more instruction, and Jonas wasn't sure whether Masoud's goal was for him to think more or to become so sleep-deprived that he stopped thinking. In between all this, Jonas read aloud an English translation of the Qur'an, focusing especially on six suras: Baqara, Al Imran, Anfal, Tawba, Rahman, and Asr. A phrase raced through Jonas's mind now: *And some people say, "We believe in Allah and the Last Day." Yet they are not believers. They seek to deceive Allah and the believers, while in fact they deceive not but their own souls.* Sura 2: 9–10.

Masoud talked a lot about self-deception and the falseness of what was generally considered reality. And souls—Jonas's soul, primarily. It turned out that talking religion endlessly was not unlike smoking weed; intense, heady, exacting, and finally exhausting. The process had strengthened Jonas's convictions. Perhaps he'd even become addicted to it in some way because now, given the final hours to be alone and settle his own mind, he felt—like a physical pressure at the base of his throat—the sharp desire for another looping dialogue with Masoud.

He began heading uptown. Bringing awareness to each precious step, he noticed how his arms and legs moved in effortless symmetry, as if in time to a nursery rhyme. One began to run through his head: *London Bridge is falling down, falling down, falling . . .* Maybe he would walk until all the anger drained away and he wearied, and then he would take the subway back downtown toward the studio apartment. Or hop a taxi if he felt like it. When Masoud took Jonas's wallet, he gave Jonas fifty bucks, like an allowance, which Jonas had in his back pocket now. At this point, why save money? Masoud had called it his emergency fund, but the irony of that almost made Jonas laugh, even at the time. The only real emergency was the one Jonas would trigger, and then miss.

He saw a woman ahead of him pausing in front of a store, the only person he'd seen hesitating on the street this morning. She was digging in a big leather purse, and when she lifted her head, he stopped short. It was his mother. God, what horrible, clumsy timing; what would he say? He felt a mounting panic.

But only for a second did she look like his mother, and then she glanced down the street, meeting his eyes, and she looked nothing like his mother, who was more fine-boned and favored flowing, rainbow-colored clothes, and besides, had reddish hair these days.

Jake and Carol. Carol and Jake. When they were young, Jonas's parents must have been something. They must have thought the very linking of their names was a prayer. They were, he imagined, so juicy once. He envisioned his mom, the bohemian potter busy at her wheel, his father, the struggling painter before the canvas, the two of them breaking from work to meet in a collision of limbs and laughter.

Jonas had a vague childhood memory of some late-night giggling between them. He remembered the curve of his mother's arm embracing both father and son. He remembered sitting at the wooden table with his father, eating slices of his mother's whole-grain bread and listening to her sing while she showered in the bathroom off the kitchen. Jake and Carol. Hippies trying to grow up in their own way.

But most of that had faded by the time he was five or six. What he remembered then was the mood in his house transitioning from steamy to sterile, which was a loss but manageable, and then to nasty, which was not. In the black period, Jonas's Sunday mornings were punctuated by the sound of yelling and the scent of bacon, which his mother said his father cooked because she hated the smell, which may have been true, since two or three strips invariably ended up in the trashcan, uneaten. After several months, the yelling gave away to a silence that vibrated, that seemed to him briefly hopeful before it was replaced by sentences that began, "Well, your *father* believes . . ." or "Your *mother* thinks . . ." Differences Jonas hadn't even known about, seemingly significant but in ways he couldn't understand, emerged in discussions that each of them had with him alone. His mother, it turned out, loved to read, while his father gravitated toward theater. His father longed to see Venice, and his mother wanted to return to Paris. His mother was a committed atheist, his father the son of Hasidic Jews. Who had known all this mattered?

Not long afterward, his father vanished from their Upper West Side apartment in one last spasm of yelling, and by the time Jonas was ten, his father owned a gallery on Lexington Avenue, with large paintings that seemed to have been thrown on the ivory walls in haste. The haphazard charm of the gallery soon attracted a throng of unconventional young art-lovers. The paintings were not by his father, as Jonas thought when he first saw them, but by artists his father represented in his new incarnation. "Up-and-coming" was the phrase his father used. His father said he did not want to paint anymore, and though both son and ex-wife understood this to be a lie, it was not discussed.

The artists whose works hung in his father's

gallery were of various ages and backgrounds, but the paintings themselves held an eerie similarity. In fact, from the beginning, walking around the gallery, Jonas could boil down his father's taste in art quite simply: whatever the frame held must have curvy lines and lots of red. Which Jonas's mother noticed, too, and somehow interpreted as a sign of materialistic misogyny, a phrase Jonas didn't even understand but which caused his father to explode: "Ridiculous!" and led to their last and most virulent argument. "You say idealism like it's a swear word now," Jonas remembered his mother shouting. After that, they stopped speaking altogether.

During this period, the boy Jonas began to get it. *You can be anything you want to be,* his parents told him, but they lied. Truth was, an enormous breach existed between one's ambitions and one's reality. "Sell-out" was a term he was still too young to know, but he began to get the general idea. His mother continued to throw pots and teach pottery classes, but it took the help of child support to keep them in their rent-controlled two-bedroom. His father occasionally showed up in society photographs, holding a glass of champagne, and his gallery remained trendy. Jonas had the sense that one was successful and the other not, but he regularly changed his mind about which parent fell into which category.

He was also a bit stunned, during the months of

divorcing, by the speed with which one could go from being part of a unit to being an individual human quite insistently separate. He later thought that if only his parents had been able to wait until he was a teenager, eager for detachment, it might have been easier on him. He might not have had the sense of betraying both of them even as they betrayed him. But by the time of the burned bacon, Jonas was already well beside the point for Carol and Jake. Just as, he guessed, Vic's little sister was beside the point now. He felt for Mara; he knew—better than Vic, he suspected—that she was having a hard time right now. He would have visited Mara once or twice more over the last few weeks if there'd been time. If things had been different.

The woman who'd reminded him of his mother had walked on, but Jonas had been standing long enough to turn cold again, so he slipped into a pharmacy and wandered up and down the artificially-lit aisles, thinking and not thinking. Images floated by: the agitated man on the bicycle outside the Peshawar madrassa, the bearded one in the training camp who'd cut a sheep's neck to prove he would not shy from necessary violence. Masoud instructing him, a hand resting on his shoulder. His mother's expression when she looked worried, his father's corny jokes. Vic, of course. Vic, with her muscular thighs and her endearing habit of touching her tongue to her upper lip when concentrating. He gave each memory and every thought a nodding but passing acknowledgment as he distracted himself by reading the backs of drugstore products, dropping some into his cart.

Then he went to the cash register and paid for the items he'd collected. He left with a packet of razors, a pair of tweezers, some nail clippers, a package of college-rule loose-leaf, a set of three blue pens, two postcards showing the Manhattan skyline, a box of business-sized envelopes, two chocolate bars, some juice, tape, a magazine, mouthwash, Saltine crackers, and first-aid cream. On his way out, he stopped at a stamp machine and bought half-a-dozen stamps, each one adorned with the image of the American flag.

At the Broadway-Lafayette stop, Vic exited and climbed to the street. On frigid days, she thought, the city's inequalities stood out in sharp relief, and she found herself wondering how Sonny Hirt survived. Most panhandlers she'd come to know by sight over the years vanished when temperatures headed south. They went someplace, she supposed, where it was easier to be homeless in winter. Sonny always stayed.

"Shouldn't you be in Florida?" she'd asked when she'd handed him a dollar earlier that day, and then she'd thought maybe the question was insensitive or he'd take offense, but Sonny had just smiled.

"You sure talking truth," he said as he shuffled on.

And so he was still working the metro, and probably would be for many hours, while she was rushing home to a warm cup of tea, warm shower, warm food. This was the kind of disparity that could set Jonas to ranting. He always felt distant problems as if they were his own, and while she could admire that, ranting was not her favorite thing about Jonas. She believed she was helping him mellow. But she suspected she was in direct competition with someone she barely knew. Jonas didn't talk about Masoud a lot, but every time he did, his admiration was obvious. She'd met Masoud once in an Italian restaurant. She listened to him speak eloquently about his home in Saudi Arabia, nights spent in the dry, crisp desert around the city, gathered with family or friends inside an open tent or sometimes outside under cloudless skies on a thick carpet, eating rice and lamb with his hands from an oversized platter shared by all. After the meal, the men played cards under the moon until the muezzin's call to morning prayer. If they couldn't make it to the mosque in time, they would stop by the roadside to pray. He made it sound romantic, timeless, and she watched Jonas's face grow more entranced as he listened to the stories.

Masoud also mentioned his older brother, who went to western Afghanistan in October 2001 to help the wounded and was killed ten days later when American rockets hit a military hospital. "My brother was a gentle and conciliatory man," Masoud said. "His life was dismissed as collateral damage." The edge of fury in his voice convinced Vic that Masoud encouraged a self-righteous, moody part of Jonas she hoped he'd outgrow.

Vic's investment in what Jonas would become was, of course, new. The camping trip changed everything. The sex had been surprising after all those years of friendship, and awkward, too, not because they were inside a tent but because they were doing it at all, touching one another in these ways. *This is Jonas,* she kept reminding herself, pausing to brush his familiar face and hands and then, like a blind woman, reaching for his unfamiliar inner thigh and the place where the small of his back had always disappeared into his jeans. She imagined he must have had the same confusing, thrilling sensation. After that first time, their lovemaking grew to feel different on different occasions. Sometimes she experienced it as a journey and lost all sense of time or place. Often it was tender. Once it was excitingly rough.

Now, on the street, she wiped her left palm on her jeans and rolled her shoulders back. Her legs were sore from the long rehearsal hours. Alex had been driving them so hard over the past week that she'd nearly lost contact with the outside world, with everything except her own dancing limbs and the members of the company. She imagined Jonas in her apartment, hopefully in just a few hours' time. She would put on an old Tina Turner CD, low—*I'm your private dancer*—and stretch him out on his back and dive her fingernails into his collarbone. Then she'd draw them gently over his chest, skirt his thighs, and move them down to the soles of his feet, like finger-painting. Imagining each finger a different shade, long strips of wavy color, all the while taking in the texture of his skin with her own. She would turn him over then and do it on the other side. Deep inside her, something coiled in anticipation.

She exhaled a puff of air made visible by the cold and experienced the deep, private happiness of knowing that in a few minutes, she would be standing in a stream of hot water, massaging her muscles with lavender-scented soap, feeling aches slide off her body. Preparing for Jonas, as she thought of it. Purifying for Jonas.

Turning the corner, she saw a woman standing on her stoop, arms crossed over her chest against the cold. Jonas's mom: that was who it looked like. But it couldn't be; what would she be doing here? Vic's fantasies about Jonas were making her imagine parts of him everywhere.

As Vic got closer, though, the woman waved, and Vic saw that it *was* Jonas's mom, which she immediately decided was a strange coincidence. Jonas's mom would never come to visit Vic—Vic doubted Jonas's mom even knew where she lived. She must be here to see someone else, someone in Vic's building, and what a fluke, here came Vic.

But no. Jonas's mom was striding toward her, one hand reaching out, saying, "Vic, hi, hon, sorry for the intrusion, I was hoping to catch you; do you have a few minutes?" For some reason, those words sent fear shooting through Vic's body, and even as Jonas's mother was in midsentence, Vic was interrupting: "Is Jonas okay? He's all right, isn't he, Mrs. Meitzner?" and before Vic could finish speaking, Jonas's mother was answering, "Carol, honey, I'm just Carol, surely, after all this time, heck, I'm not even married to Mr. Meitzner anymore, and yes, Jonas is fine, at least I think so, I mean, nothing's happened, nothing specific, but that's what I want to talk with you about."

Vic was so startled she couldn't even think of how to respond properly, and then she realized they were still on the street, where it continued to be frigid, and then she wondered how messy her place was—Mrs. Meitzner kept a neat apartment, she knew—but how could she even think of that? How many times over the years, during high school and beyond, had Mrs. Meitzner welcomed her, made her dinner, even insisted that Jonas walk her home if it got too late?

"Come on in," Vic said. "Yes, please. I'm just surprised. I didn't even know that you knew my address—"

"Your mom . . . I called . . ."

Vic unlocked the first door to the building, and then the second door, and Mrs. Meitzner followed her up three flights, and Vic unlocked the apartment door and flung it open to the living room, which wasn't too cluttered, a pair of boots by the door, a plate, a coffee cup and a partially read newspaper on the floor in front of the couch, two wineglasses on a table to the side, and a small pile of clothes in the corner. "What can I get you to drink, Mrs. Meitzner? I have some herbal tea?"

"That would be perfect on a day like this, thank you, but please call me Carol, okay?"

Vic nodded mutely, and they both stepped into the open kitchen—really just a counter, a stovetop, an oven, and some cabinets for glasses and dishes.

Vic put on the water and pulled out three boxes of tea bags so Jonas's mother could choose, and while they fussed together in the kitchen, Jonas's mother asked about the dance company, and how practice was going, and when the performance would be, and how Vic's parents were, and Vic answered on autopilot, wondering all the while what this could be about. She wondered if Jonas's mother knew about the unexpected outcome of the camping trip, and how it had changed the status between Jonas and Vic, and if she would say, "You're not good enough for my son; stay away from him." But those were lines from some B movie, and Jonas's mother was nothing like that; she was much more tolerant and classy. Besides, she liked Vic; Vic was sure of that; she always had.

Freshman year. Jonas and Vic were in a physical science class together. He'd skipped a grade and was the smartest kid in that class, but he didn't look the part. Jonas was not nerdy. Yet he had the face of a scholar. His eyes were set a little too close together for beauty, but it was the ideal flaw because it made him look focused. Which he was.

He also had no idea how attractive his shyness made him. And then there was his curly blond hair—who could resist that?

Vic already loved dance, and that contributed to her indifference as a student. She was one of those *you-have-such-potential* students. When she needed help in science, as she inevitably did, she asked the guy who sat two seats in front of her. Jonas. She found out they lived near one another, and that was how they started. Study partners. Two times a week for the rest of that year, and they kept it up over the next three years. In the beginning, Vic was sure heads bent over a book would develop into something else. And then Jonas didn't seem interested, which surprised her. Vic was accustomed to boys' interest. But she accepted Jonas's indifference. He was too moody and serious for her, anyway, she decided; she had wild oats to sow. Besides, he was a great friend. She was glad to have him for that. Still, every now and then she would become aware of the golden skin of his forearm or the way his back curved sweetly before it reached toward his legs, and a lusty thought would pass lazily through her mind. But mostly, before August, she'd just thought of him as study-buddy, steady-buddy Jonas.

Finally with the tea ready, Vic puffed up the pillows on the couch and the two women sat together. Vic couldn't call Jonas's mother Carol, so she decided to just call her nothing. They pointed their knees in each other's direction, and Vic waited.

Jonas's mother sipped her tea, then took a deep breath. "I feel a little silly," she said, stumbling over her words a bit. "I've been worried, and maybe I worry too much, but then I thought, *Well, if anyone would know, it would be Vic,* because you two are so close and you've been that way for so long."

She looked expectantly at Vic, but so far there was nothing for Vic to reply to, so she just nodded encouragingly, aware of her heart moving up into her throat even though she couldn't say why.

"Well, okay, here's the thing, I don't know, Vic, but I don't think he's going to any classes anymore, even though he told me a couple weeks ago that he was. And Jonas doesn't normally lie to me, at least I don't think so."

"I . . . I *thought* he was going to classes," Vic said. She knew Jonas considered many of the classes to be "dishonest"; that was how he'd put it. But he hadn't mentioned to her that he wasn't attending at all. It wasn't impossible to imagine. Jonas had already dropped out once, midway through freshman year. He'd spent a year traveling around Europe—the United Kingdom, Sweden, Norway, Italy, and France—and then he'd returned and begun to work at that center he loved so much—the World Understanding Center or something like that—answering phones and preparing class cards in return for a small salary. He studied comparative religion and meditation there, Ayurvedic medicine, Kabbalah and Sufism and who could keep track of what else—searching for something, a quality Vic found endearing. Then his parents insisted he start classes at NYU full time again in September. It seemed to be going pretty well, although, come to think of it, he never mentioned classes. But after all, it had only been—what? Ten weeks? They'd had other matters on their minds, the two of them.

"It's not only that," Jonas's mother said. "He's been strange, distant. Oh, I know it's normal for young men to pull away from their mothers. But this feels bigger than that. I mean, I can't reach him, and . . ." She pulled a little on the fabric of the couch. "He came over two weeks ago, and he didn't look good," she said, almost as if she were speaking to herself, her gaze on some middle distance. "His face was gray. He carried his body like it weighed a hundred tons, though he looked like he'd actually lost weight. I asked him how he felt. He said fine. 'Any fatigue or anything?' He turned angry suddenly. He called me a nag—" She cut herself off, and Vic could see a flash of hurt in her expression before it cleared. "Later he was in his room—his old room, I mean—he was looking out the window, and I came and stood behind him and grabbed his waist, tried to scare him, playfully, you know, and I guess I did scare him because he jumped and turned. He was hanging on to that old stuffed elephant of his, and he looked so worn. God, he looked ancient."

Jonas's mother's eyes were shiny. She took a sip of tea. Vic thought about patting her hand, but that seemed the wrong gesture between them. "You know how he is," Vic said. "Sometimes he carries around the world's problems like an overstuffed suitcase."

Jonas's mother didn't seem to hear. "I asked him what was wrong. He said nothing, and then he got mad again, then apologetic, one right after the other. Then he left."

Vic sipped her tea. "Well," she said after a minute.

"I know." Jonas's mother ran a hand through her hair and kind of laughed. "Oh, I know, it doesn't add up to much, the way I've told it. But a mother can sense things. Something is wrong." She worried the fabric of Vic's couch a moment more, hesitating. "Do you think, could it be *drugs* or something?"

Vic smiled; she even felt some relief because this was beginning to feel like a typical parent conversation. "No, Mrs. Meitzner. Jonas doesn't even drink."

"Of course. You're right. But something is . . ." Jonas's mom trailed off and reached her left hand back to rub the right side of her neck. "For three days, I've been calling, leaving messages, and he doesn't answer and he doesn't call back. That's not like him, either. And today I went by his apartment and—no answer. So I thought maybe . . . maybe you would know something. When did you last talk to him?"

"I think it was . . ." She'd thought of Jonas often, for sure, and made repeated calls, but how long exactly had it been since they'd spoken? With dance rehearsals, and then the drama with her mother and Mara, the days had begun to blur. She couldn't sort it out right now, not with Jonas's mom staring at her. "Last time I talked to him," she said, "he seemed—" Tired, maybe, and busy, but mostly he'd seemed romantic every time she'd spoken to him over these past few weeks. And intense, and passionate. And full of life and desire and longing, and now she suddenly remembered the last time, a week ago Tuesday—longer than she'd realized. It had been a quick conversation, and she'd been on the street headed to rehearsal, but still she'd felt it all when she'd heard his voice on the phone, and she'd wanted to see him, to hold his face in her hands, and would have found a way to do that, to meet him at least on some street corner and kiss him, kiss him in some private place, if she hadn't already been late. "He seemed fine," she said.

"Okay. Well, good," Jonas's mother said, though she sounded unconvinced. She was silent a moment and then made a motion as if dusting off the palms of her hands on her pants. "Enough. You've probably got plenty to do on a Sunday afternoon."

"No, no," Vic said.

Jonas's mother rose and took her cup into the kitchen, set it in the sink. "He was such a funny baby," she said. "So serious, even then. But one time, he was maybe eleven months then, and he was sitting in his high chair in the kitchen, and suddenly, out of nowhere, he started laughing, and that made me laugh, and then he laughed at me laughing, and on like that, as if the laughter itself were an entire conversation." She gave a small, sad smile. "If you . . ." she hesitated, "if you talk to Jonas in the next day or so, Vic—I don't want to sound pathetic, but tell him to call his old mother, okay?"

As soon as she was gone, Vic tried Jonas again on his cell. It went immediately to the message, so he either had it off or was underground somewhere. She tried to remember whether it had rung when she'd called him from the theater. She dialed his apartment phone, and there was no answer—but she knew he rarely answered his landline; it was just something his parents had asked him to do, to put in a phone. She called his cell again to leave a message.

"Hey, you, it's me. Me on Sunday afternoon. Maybe you have time for an early dinner tonight? Even if you don't, call me, okay? Your mom was here, which was a surprise, but nice, except that she thinks you've dropped out of sight for too long. She's worried, Jonas. Give her a call. And then, busy or not, call *me*." She hung up and then dialed Jonas's number again. "If I don't answer, I'm in the shower. So leave a message. Or better yet," she dropped her voice, trying for comic-seductive, "come on over. Quickly."

She sat cross-legged on the floor for a minute, trying to remember one of their most recent conversations. A couple weeks ago he'd taken a few bites out of a graham cracker and tried to persuade her that it resembled a person's head, and then he'd made it into a talking man begging to be inside her stomach, and she'd giggled and opened her mouth wide and eaten the man entirely. Sometimes they talked about places they wanted to visit, a favorite topic. Sometimes they shared details about past lovers—lovers they'd known about back in the days when they'd been only friends, but then they hadn't listened for quite the same details, or with quite the same attention.

He told her about a girl in Sweden, who didn't seem to mean much, and another in Ireland— Deirdre was her name, and she made a stronger impression. Jonas grew so concentrated while recalling her. He didn't talk about the way she looked or her temperament. He talked about her past. During the Troubles, when Deirdre was eighteen, she drove a bomb-laden car for the IRA from Belfast to some nearby town and parked it near a police station. She left the car and took a bus, and by the time she arrived home, she flipped on the news to find that the car bomb had detonated, killing several people.

"A terrorist? Your girlfriend was a terrorist?"

"One man's terrorist . . ." Jonas began.

"But really," Vic said. "People died."

Jonas shook his head. "She had this . . . conviction, maturity. She was twelve years older than me, but it wasn't her age; it was how committed she was to her decisions. Made me feel like a kid."

"Didn't she feel guilty?" The whole topic made Vic uneasy. She couldn't tell if her unease was fueled by simple jealousy or something else, but she hoped Jonas would pronounce some judgment against this Deirdre to make her feel safer.

"Only difference between the statesman and the terrorist leader," he said, "is that one is still in a position of weakness, while the other is part of the government. Sometimes it takes physical force to prevent an issue from vanishing."

Jonas's eyes had a faraway look that made Vic long to bring him back, so she climbed on top of him. "Okay. Physical force. So this issue. Doesn't vanish," she said, and began kissing him, pulling him away from those old-girlfriend memories and returning him to the moment with her.

Vic was the more experienced in the arena of lovemaking; they'd both always known that. She'd wondered if this might make Jonas jealous, but it seemed only to make him laugh. Once, after they'd rolled together on the bed, almost like children, for hours, he sprang up naked and knelt on the floor and bowed a few times and said, "Thank you to all your previous lovers, because everything they taught you, I am now gathering that fruit and it sustains my life." She laughed and pulled him back to bed, wrapping her legs around him again.

Once not so long ago, he held her hand over his chest, spread her fingers out, and they lay there breathing together, matching each inhalation and exhalation, alert but as still as if they were jointly meditating. He seemed about to tell her something, even began speaking a word she couldn't make out, but then he broke off. She didn't press him because she figured it was about them. About the unexpected quality of this romance, its intensity and resonance. He'd already said some of that, once or twice. She smiled, thinking of it, and wished he were here right now, sprawled on her couch.

She was more circumspect than Jonas in expressing her emotions. Experience had taught her that what seemed real was too often revealed to be false. She'd learned that lesson early in high school, observing her friends who claimed to be "in love," and her skepticism was only reinforced by her parents' split, which Vic knew, even if neither her mother nor Mara did, had been a long time in coming. Maybe as a consequence, whenever Vic began to feel strong attachment, her throat invariably grew tight, making endearments reluctant to emerge and awkward when they did. It was as if vulnerability caused a physical reaction that left her close to inarticulate. Jonas never complained about her reticence; he never even mentioned it.

But maybe she'd been too guarded this time. She didn't need, after all, to get caught up in considering the future, what would and wouldn't be, what might *change,* as her mother had warned, because this moment was what existed now, and for this moment, it was good—better than good. Besides, this was Jonas. She trusted him, had trusted him even before. And now, when she was with him, she felt something that had been clenched within her opening, wide and wider, causing a delicious sensation, the sensation of possibility. Greater courage in the face of emotional exposure: maybe that was what Jonas could teach her, because in this arena, she was a virgin. So maybe next time she saw him—maybe tonight, in fact, in the midst of ravaging his sweet body—she would bypass her caution, put her hands on his heart, and let him know what depths she held inside.

The first thing Mara needed was a subway map, because if she intended to get up very early, she should be clear beforehand on where exactly she was headed. It would be nice if she could have her father's precise address, but she didn't know that and didn't know how to get it. She could ask neither her mother nor her father because the simple request would involve too many questions that she didn't want to answer, not now. She planned to get in the general vicinity of her father's new apartment, come aboveground, and call him on her cell phone. He would rush out to the street to meet her, and he would offer to make her pancakes or buy her a bagel, and over breakfast, he'd hear her out. Thankfully, she at least knew his cross streets. He'd given her the names in the one real exchange they'd had about his moving out, a conversation held at a neighborhood café where he'd taken her for a chocolate croissant. Until then, chocolate croissants had been her favorite; now just the sight of them nauseated her.

"We don't know how long it will be for," he'd said in response to her first question. "We'll just see, and I don't want you to worry, and of course I'm still your father," he'd waved his hand, "and your mother is your mother, all that, you know.

You'll come and see me soon, I hope. And you know, little angel—you're such a smart girl—you know nothing is your fault. Nothing is anyone's fault, in fact. No one is to blame, and I'm not sure anyone ever is." Then he'd covered her hand with his and stared into her eyes. "Do you understand?"

Mara had looked around uncomfortably. Customers were sitting at three other tables, but they all seemed fully involved in their own dialogues. The waitress, though, was clearly watching this little drama between Mara and her father. Casually combing her hair with the fingers of her left hand, she watched with knowing, though only mildly interested, eyes—probably happened every week, some guilty dad brought his kids in for chocolate croissants and the Talk, and here was another one, and maybe it would mean a good tip, because wasn't there some connection between guilt and money that could end up benefiting everyone at moments like this, even observers who did nothing more than refresh the water?

"Sometimes what we want changes," Mara's father had said. "Now, that I know you can understand." He ran a hand across his forehead as though wiping away invisible sweat. "Let's see," he said. "When you were four years old—here's a good example—you wanted a blue hat. You wanted a blue straw hat more than anything in the world. That's the exact expression you used with your mother and me. I think you must have seen a picture somewhere, or maybe you conjured it up in your own mind, but it was November, your birthday, and blue straw hats were hard to come by. Blue straw is an Easter hat, not one for Thanksgiving." He chuckled, but Mara just watched him, silent. "Well, anyway, we searched every where. Finally we found one in a children's clothing store in the Village. We had to ask—it wasn't on display, but they had one leftover and sitting in the back room, and they brought it out and it was sky blue and your mother and I almost yelped with happiness. And now, where is that blue hat? Who knows? It doesn't matter. I mean, it does, but you've changed and you've grown and you wanted it then but you want other things now. And that's as it should be. That's healthy."

Mara glanced away from her father, looking out the window. She did know where the blue hat was—stuck in the corner of the shelf inside her closet. And actually, she did still love it. But she knew she was being nitpicky, unwilling to concede anything to her father and intentionally refusing to absorb his argument when in fact it was true that she no longer wanted the blue hat with the desperation that her father had described, if she'd ever wanted it that way. She just kept it. She kept it fondly. But she would never wear it again.

After staring out the window long enough to

make a point about how she wouldn't be won over by some memory, some childhood story that demonstrated her parents' previous attentiveness, she turned back to her father. "So, where *do* you live now?"

He chuckled a little again. Guilt, it turned out, made him tolerant of Mara's belligerent tone. "Off Kingston, near St. Johns," he'd said. "Across the bridge, in Brooklyn, but it's still very close and you'll come see my apartment soon and if you want, I can draw you a map right now."

She'd refused, which she wished now she hadn't, but she'd asked him to spell the names of the streets and he'd taken out a pen and written them down on a napkin: "Kingston" and "St. Johns," and she'd put the napkin in her pocket, and he'd smiled as though something were settled between them, as though he'd accomplished what he'd set out to do, and soon after, they left the café. At home, she put the napkin under her pillow so she could sleep on those two words, as though she were bringing Kingston and St. Johns into this apartment, bringing her father home.

Her mother did not have any metro maps in the apartment. Her mother knew the metro system, and if she didn't know something, she looked at the maps posted underground, in the stations themselves. Her mother never kept unnecessary paperwork in the house. Her father sometimes took days, even weeks, to read the *New York*

Times, but her mother was religious about trying to throw away magazines and Vic's and Mara's graded school papers and notes scrawled on scraps of paper as soon as she could get away with it. Once, thinking about this, Mara decided it was because her mother worked with so many papers in her job, always editing one manuscript or another, that she needed to keep them to a minimum at home. But then she realized her father worked with the same number of papers, and stacks of paper didn't bother him, even seemed to please him. So she stopped thinking about it.

Mara's mother was in her room when Mara called through the door, "Mom? I'm going downstairs to see Aaron. Okay?"

Her mother opened the bedroom door. "Oh, honey," she said. "I've been such bad company today. Yes, go see Aaron. Great. Good. Just come back up in time for dinner, okay?"

Mara wasn't allowed to go many places by herself. Her parents or Vic or some other adult always accompanied her, even to the corner to buy something for school from the stationery store. "You're too small," her mother often said. "Someone could pick you up and walk away with you in a second." So Aaron's was about the only place Mara was allowed to go on her own, and that had probably made them better friends than they might have been. Now Mara walked down three flights instead of taking the elevator. She knew

Aaron would be home on a Sunday afternoon, and she knew Aaron would have a subway map, or if he didn't, he would still be able to tell her how to get to Kingston and St. Johns.

Aaron answered the door, and his mother was right behind him, saying, "Oh, hi, Mara, come on in." Mara smiled and nodded but gave Aaron a quick, meaningful look so he would know she didn't want to sit in the kitchen and eat a snack and chat with his mother. She wanted to go to his room fast so they could talk privately.

Aaron was twelve, a year older than Mara, and a genius about the New York City subway system. While other boys outgrew their fascination with trains by middle school, for Aaron it had become an obsession, an alternate reality. He still kept train tracks under his bed. His favorite clothes were those that bore the emblems of subway lines. And he knew the history of the metro system as well as he knew the shape of his own body. Given the slightest encouragement, he would reveal that the first underground line had opened in New York City in 1904, that they had sliced open the sidewalk in order to build the tunnel and then reconstructed it. "Like open-heart surgery," he liked to say. He knew how much certain lines had cost, and he could recall off the top of his head subway crime statistics over the years. It was all organized in his mind like a computer, and to Mara it was so amazing that it made up for the fact that Aaron was a little bit nerdy and not in possession of much in the way of humor.

"What subway do I have to take to get from here into Brooklyn, to St. Johns and Kingston?" Mara asked as soon as Aaron closed the door to his bedroom.

"Hmm," he said. For a few minutes, he studied a map of all the boroughs that took up one wall in his bedroom. "Here it is," he said finally. "The Utica Avenue stop on the number 4 would be best, I think. Atlantic Center is a mix of trains. There may be other ways you could do it. The S-train, for example. Is this weekend or weekday? Is it before or after midnight?"

"Weekday. About 6 A.M.," she said.

He turned away from the map and looked at her without speaking for a moment. "This isn't theoretical, then?"

"What did you think, I wanted to know for a social studies test or something?" Mara asked, though not unkindly.

Aaron took off his glasses, cleaned both lenses on his T-shirt, and replaced them on his face. "What *do* you need to know for?"

"My dad," Mara said. "That's where he's living now."

Aaron nodded knowingly. Aaron knew all about Mara's parents—or at least, as much as Mara knew. His own father, a surgeon, had lived apart from his mother as long as Aaron could remember, so Aaron considered that normal, and that was why Mara knew she could tell him about her parents and have someone to talk with who would be matter-of-fact about what felt to her like an earthquake.

"I could tell you how to get there," Aaron said. "I could give you a few ways. But your dad will show you."

"I'm not going with my dad," Mara said.

Aaron sat down on his bed. "Your mom?" he asked.

"No, and not Vic, either. I'm going alone."

"When?"

"Tomorrow. I'm going to see my dad and tell him how it is, and I'm going to . . ." Mara broke off, suddenly thinking she might cry and knowing Aaron could hear that possibility in her voice.

Aaron stood up awkwardly. "You want a glass of water?" he asked as he headed for the door, and he didn't wait for an answer. When he returned a minute later, Mara was fine; she didn't need the water and didn't even want to take it, but Aaron held it out.

"Thanks," she said.

"What time are we going?" he asked.

"We?"

He nodded.

"What about school?"

"Yes," he said. "What about school?"

She smiled. She almost wanted to hug Aaron.

"I'm going to be late for school," she said. "I'm figuring my mom will understand."

"And I guess you and your dad are going to want to talk without me, but maybe I can sit in the kitchen or something. Does he have a kitchen?"

"Yes. Probably. I mean, I don't know, but doesn't everyone have a kitchen?"

"Okay," Aaron said. "I'll set my alarm and meet you outside your door."

"What'll you tell your mom?'

Aaron tipped his head. "I'll tell her I'm meeting a friend early at school to study. She'll be so happy I *have* a friend that she won't ask more." He took the water glass from her and set it on his window ledge. He stood in front of the piano they kept in his room and banged a couple keys. "Hey," he said, "what time do you have to be home?"

"Dinnertime."

"Okay, so . . . you want to watch *The French Connection* before dinner?"

She didn't because she'd already seen it with him twice. But she knew he loved watching New York subway scenes in movies, and he especially loved *The French Connection* with the hit man trying to escape on the subway car, and Mara figured she owed him. Besides, she could pretend; she knew how to do that. She could pretend to enjoy it again. So she nodded, "Yeah, sure," and managed to grin as she followed him to the corner of the living room where they kept the DVD player, and he found the movie and they sank together onto the couch, Aaron looking as full of anticipation as if it were the first time, his expression alone enough to make Mara's grin real.

Before submerging into the subway station, Carol
fumbled in her pocket to pull out her cell phone,
hoping for a missed call from Jonas. Instead she
found a text from Lorenzo: "Dinner 2nite?
Seafood? Bizness only, if u insist." The message
made her smile, though only briefly. Lorenzo was
a source of guilt right now. They'd met six months
ago when she, musing over the ways her life could
or should change now that Jonas had long since
moved out, had applied for a job as a teacher at an
upscale pottery studio Lorenzo owned, one connected to a Manhattan spa. He'd been complimen-
tary, and then interested, and then romantic, and
she'd lost her head. It had been the first time in a
long time, something she'd rarely permitted herself when Jonas was younger. For a few weeks,
she'd been the one out of touch and so hadn't been
paying attention to her son just when, her intuition
now suggested, she should have been. Mothering
was a lifetime, full-time job.

"Maybe. Let's talk later," she texted back. She
had no desire to tell him about her Jonas-related
fears. So far their relationship had been carefree,
almost child-like. She couldn't imagine Lorenzo
as a partner in the problems of real life. She
returned her cell phone to her pocket, took a last

look into the pale sky that hovered above the city, and then headed down the subway steps, littered with discarded MetroCards like golden autumn leaves, memories from trips taken, time gone by.

Jonas didn't know about Lorenzo but probably wouldn't care if he did. What *would* anger him was Carol's visit to Vic's. He'd consider it inexcusably intrusive. He'd say she'd crossed a line, taking her fears to his friends. She was acting out of concern, but she also had to admit that what she longed for, what she missed with a poignancy that ached in some dense middle part of her, was the easy intimacy she'd shared with Jonas for years. They'd always gotten along well, until recently. None of the typical teenage trials or rebellions. Their relationship revolved around shared conversations and meals and movies and books.

He'd been a talker practically from birth. When Jonas was a toddler, she used to say, "Let's listen to music for a little while, sweetie," just to take a break from his babbling voice. He kept talking, even as he got older. When he was depressed, his voice grew deep and heavy; when he was angered by perceived injustices in the world, he grew loud, but he didn't stop talking. Even after he moved out, he called or dropped in, and usually he was like a faucet she couldn't turn off even if she'd wanted to. So when their conversation had suddenly dried up a few months ago, she'd felt her own loneliness like a lumpy, dust-filled couch she'd owned so long that she'd almost stopped seeing it, only now there it was, an eyesore in the middle of the room, too cumbersome to move.

She could admit all that, but loneliness was not what had driven her to Vic's door. She was willing, she *was,* to let Jonas go and to let her life move on to the next stage, challenges and all. What she was unwilling to do was live with this fearful feeling that clung to her like a bad scent, a worry frustratingly undefined but so strong she'd woken up a dozen times in the middle of the night, wrapped in murky dreams or covered in goose bumps, sensing something was wrong.

Ever since adolescence, Jonas had suffered from periods of overcast internal weather. He asked for so much from life. He demanded the stripping away of the skin; he insisted on seeing all the way to the muscles and veins, but if those muscles seemed insubstantial, the veins too paltry to carry the essential rush of blood, he was as disappointed as an old man finished with his days. At those times, when he spoke, his voice would catch on some random word, as if everything was about to be too much for him. Sometimes, in those depression periods, she felt Jonas was almost lost to her, wandering alone in a bitter night, carrying only a flashlight with a beam too hesitant and shallow to guide him home.

She swiped her MetroCard and entered the station. Two cops lingered near the turnstile, chatting and stamping their feet to keep warm in the clammy underground. A young woman with pierced lip and baby carriage stood at the top of the stairs leading down one level to the uptown A and C. "Need help?" Carol asked.

The woman gave a loud sigh. "See, that's what I'm talking about," she said, tipping her head toward the police officers. "Not a single uniform steps up. Takes a ma'am to offer." Carol smiled, taking hold of the carriage's front end, and together the two women descended, carting the carriage and the sleeping baby inside.

"Boy?" Carol asked, leaning over to look at the tiny, fresh face of the well-bundled infant.

The woman nodded.

"How old?"

"Ten months."

"Keeping you up nights?"

The woman shrugged. "Sleeps all right. And thank the Lord, 'cause I got work in the morning, and no idea where his father is anymore." She reached to stroke the infant's cheek. "This sweet baby the single sole best thing that man and I ever did together."

"You know . . ." Carol hesitated. "Well, it's a cliché."

The woman cocked her head. "What?"

"About it going fast. But my God, it goes fast." Carol took a deep breath. "I have a boy, too."

"Yes?" The woman looked at Carol through narrowed eyes. "How old?"

"Oh, old. Old. But I still remember. . . . *We* change, but they change more."

Carol suddenly couldn't say anything more; her voice would have been drowned out anyway by two trains approaching on parallel tracks, each going the opposite direction. The trains shuddered to a halt and paused before the doors swung open simultaneously. The woman was headed one direction, Carol the other. "You take care, now," the woman said.

These unexpected intersections of lives: she loved them. Did it make her pathetic that at least once a month, a conversation shared with someone on a subway ended up being the highlight of her day? She loved the subway, too, for being such an equalizer. Some moments couldn't be romanticized: the morning the hungover young man, slumped in a seat across from her, suddenly straightened and threw up on her shoes, for instance. Nevertheless, it was the world's finest people-watching gallery and a classroom in tolerance. Where else could a suited businessman sit between a homeless derelict and an immigrant Chinese tailor? Forget Broadway and Times Square. It was the subway that displayed New York at its best, its forbearance, its liveliness, its effort to overcome the Tower of Babel collapse of a common tongue. For all its flaws, the subway was the city's jewel.

The train was nearly full, but she got a seat next to a teenage boy listening to music through earphones. Many of the passengers, by chance, were parents with children—or maybe she just found herself noticing them. Across from her, a father with a broad, Irish-looking face sat next to a little boy who looked very much like his miniature, both of them expressionless. Next to him, a woman in traditional Islamic dress held a babe in arms.

Initially Jake had been the one who'd pressed for a baby; Carol had wavered, her concerns like stripes on a feminist flag. What if she lost her independence? What if she became just someone's mom? What if her own work vanished beneath diapers and report cards and high school dances? But then: Jonas. He'd been such an empathetic child, feeling everything from Carol's pain at the breakup to the loss of a belly-up goldfish that had to be flushed.

So of course, with all this sensitivity, when he reached adolescence, he began questioning. He went through periods of doubting the values of everyone around him, from the principal of his school to the director of his theater group to the artists Jake represented, and finally to her, his mom. And she was fine with that. She could stand up to a bit of close examination, she told herself; she wasn't that bad. Besides, how much worse if she'd raised a little Republican who bought into it all without any reservations?

Still, it was hard to see him so confused and then disturbed and ultimately angered by the compromises people had to make in order to get along in the modern material world. At least, the compromises they made in the West, and in America, and in New York City, and on his block, and in his home.

"We're all terrorists," he'd told her a few weeks ago in what had been their last real conversation. "Every single one of us. The only difference is, some of us recognize it and others don't."

She'd started to disagree with him, to explain the falseness built into the very extremity of that viewpoint, how it held many accountable for the actions of few and failed to take into account the moderating influence of community and family, let alone one's own personal honorable efforts to control rage, be kind, make amends. Then she'd decided not to argue. This perspective sprang from nothing more than the rashness and absolutism of youth. He'd outgrow it. She thought about getting him a T-shirt imprinted with the slogan: "I'm twenty-one. This isn't who I really am" but discarded the idea. It was so true—he would be very different in another decade—and once he might have recognized the truth in it. He might have laughed. Now she wasn't sure.

Truth be told, part of what nagged at her now was a fear that he'd stopped calling not out of forgetfulness or busyness but as an intentional act, that he'd lumped her in with all the rest, all those he thought were shells of beings, committing or acceding to violence in their half-sleep; those he disdained; those he was sure he would never resemble. And though she knew they could survive this, the two of them, and that he would mature and pass through it, still it hurt, and it worried her not to know what he was thinking.

Three stops from her own, she heard a panhandler giving his spiel at the other end of the train. "If you ain't got it, I understand, 'cause I ain't got it. But if you have a dime, a quarter, a piece of fruit . . ."

She didn't normally give to panhandlers—there were too many of them, and who knew what they used the money for? She had her own favorite charities. But now, because she was worried about her son and because she knew Jonas would pull something out of his pocket to give to this man if he were here, she fished into her bag for a dollar.

"Yes, ma'am," the boy next to her said with a grin as he stretched out a leg to reach into his own jeans pocket. "We def got to give it up for Sonny Hirt."

"That's his name?"

"Huh?" The boy removed one earphone and let it dangle over his shoulder.

"His name is *Sunny Hurt?* Really?" she asked. "That sounds like a contradiction."

The boy looked at her curiously. "You never seen Sonny before? He's an institution, yo."

The panhandler shuffled forward. He had warm eyes. Carol thought of this man's mother, who'd surely doted on him when he was a baby, had probably worried herself sick when he was an adolescent. Had he been wild? Done drugs, cut school? Had that been when everything began going wrong? Or had it been much later, after he'd had a job, maybe even a wife? Something had fallen apart. Maybe distrust of the system, not unlike what Jonas felt.

At her stop, she emerged from the train to see two more officers; this was a lot for a Sunday, and she wondered if someone special were in town, visiting the UN or dining with the mayor. Police officers barely looked at her now—middle-aged, middle-class white women were virtually invisible to them, off the radar, unlikely to be criminals and too old for flirting. When she was young and running around with Jake, it was a different matter. They'd both looked free and flamboyant in those days, they'd looked like trouble, and to top it off, they were always laughing. Carol used to feel police officers following her and Jake with their eyes, suspicious, waiting from them to slip up somehow.

Jake. There it was, the thought she'd been avoiding, because she knew. It was time for Jake. This worry about Jonas was too strong, and she needed to share it with Jonas's father. Jake used to be a little intuitive, and so, who knew, maybe he'd felt something, too. Or maybe Jonas had confided something in him, although that would be a switch. Still, every other path had dead-ended. As soon as she got home, she'd fix herself a cup of tea but also pour something stronger so she could take a sip if Jake became obnoxious. And then she'd call him. It was time to talk to Jake about her worries over the best thing they'd ever done together.

In the back office of his gallery, Jake's laptop was open to Craig's List, missed connections on the subway, his favorite frivolous reading.

No. 5 Train to Bowling Green: You were wearing light brown boots, and something green on top. I was the guy with glasses. We sort of exchanged glances through the people standing in the subway car. You were awfully cute and I don't see many gals with your sort of style around here. Maybe lunch? Or more?

Last Friday night on the downtown F-train. Me: The brunette with the low-cut black dress whose chest you kept staring at (yes, I noticed). You: Light brown hair with goatee, blue shirt, and more of a chance than you gave yourself credit for. Wanna see 'em in person? So holler back, cutie!

He didn't have a goatee, but maybe he could still respond to that one—nah, he surely hadn't sunk to that. He pushed the laptop away and had begun running his finger down a row of figures on a spreadsheet when the phone rang. He reached for it immediately, pleased for another distraction from issues of money and also tantalized by the possibility that the caller might be bearing good business news. Maybe a client wanted to buy a piece from a recent show—one of the big paintings, please God, because would that ever take a weight off. Or maybe it was a new artist, some undiscovered talent looking for a place to hang his work. Even if it were only one of his regular artists checking on sales, that was fine; Jake would strike up a conversation that might lead somewhere productive—at least more productive than reviewing financials, or even reviewing Craig's List.

He glanced at the phone number casually and then held the receiver away from his ear. 212-566-1382. *His* number. Or rather, his old number. Or rather, Carol's number, now that Jonas didn't live there anymore. And Carol didn't call him, not ever.

He put down the receiver without answering, and, waiting to see if she'd leave a message, he let his eyes rest on the painting in his office. It was a cityscape, showing Manhattan's skyscrapers as though they were on fire and beneath them a red curve that was the Hudson. It was not one of his favorites; he preferred more abstract, but he always rotated paintings in and out of his office so that none of his artists would feel slighted.

Either she wasn't leaving a message, or it was a very long one. He waited another minute, and the phone began to ring again. Damn her. She knew he was here, somehow. She had this extra sense when it came to family members, even ex–family members, apparently, and she wasn't going to let up. He answered the phone.

"Hello, Carol," he said.

"Jake." Her voice sounded deep and husky, and God save him if it didn't bring back a rush of memories; God save him if he couldn't suddenly imagine her, twenty-one years old, on her back by the lake that one afternoon, her traffic-stopping legs askew; God save him if he didn't recall the precise and precious taste of her and that tiny, pristine hotel room in the French Quarter the time they barely saw the city, and the intoxicating night they slipped away from a fancy summer party and made love behind the cabana and again in the shallow end of the swimming pool, and even that time right near the end when they passed in the hallway after another fight and abruptly found themselves doing it jammed into the bathroom while Jonas slept.

"It's Jonas," she said.

"Jonas?" Jake felt sluggish, like he was being awakened from a dream. "Jonas? What's happened? What's wrong?"

"Nothing; he's fine, I mean, I think so; at least, it's nothing specific," she said. "It's just that he's, oh, God, Jake. Something's going on, even though I'm having trouble articulating it here. He's in trouble, or troubled—I don't know what because he's been, well, he's been not-Jonas." Carol paused, and it sounded like she took a sip of a drink. "I think he's cutting classes," she said. "He hasn't called me. I call; there's no answer. I went to his apartment today, and he wasn't there. I haven't heard from him in more than a week."

"How much more than a week?"

"It's been nine days."

"Carol." Jake leaned back in his chair. "Nine days?"

"So I guess you haven't spoken with him any more recently than that?"

"I hadn't really thought about it, but no, I guess not. I wasn't particularly worried, though."

"This is Jonas. It isn't like him not to call one of us—usually me, granted, but at least one of us—for this long."

Jake decided to ignore Carol's slightly snide tone. "Yes, this is Jonas," he said, "but this is Jonas growing up. I mean, my God, he's twenty-one. Isn't he?" Jake calculated quickly. "That's right. So it's time."

"Jake," she said. "Something is wrong, I *know* something is wrong, and I don't know what to do."

Jake sighed. "Do you remember," he said, "when you and I began seeing one another?"

"Jake," she said, and he knew by her tone that she thought maybe he was going to begin with the sex talk, which he used to do sometimes when they had to be apart, and which he did a few especially lonely times after they split. But it had been years, and besides, even he wouldn't do that now. Not when they were talking about their boy. Not when she was so distracted.

"It was all new, Carol. Every time we touched one another, every word we exchanged. It was all we could think about, all we could feel. Neither one of us was keeping in close contact with our *mothers*."

"Jonas is neither you nor I. He's something else altogether, something so pure and fine and idealistic and . . . and when he stops calling for this long, something is wrong."

"Pure and idealistic is all well and good, but Carol, he can still be in the throes of some lustful relationship—"

"I went by Vic's," Carol said. "That's how worried I am, Jake, so hear me out. I went by Vic's, even at the risk of sounding like the crazy possessive mother, but Vic didn't know anything, either."

"Vic?"

"You know. His friend from high school."

Jake wasn't a hundred percent sure if Vic was male or female, but he decided to keep that piece of ignorance to himself. He stood up with the receiver tucked against his ear and peeked into the gallery. Except for Sundays and Thursdays, when he invited the public, he was opening the gallery these days only for shows and by appointment. He hadn't heard the bell that signaled the door opening, but he thought he might have missed it. He hadn't, though. No potential buyer was browsing the paintings; no one had been browsing

121

so far all day, which was not good for a Sunday, even a cold Sunday, especially given the figures he'd just been studying.

"Carol," he said, "what do you want me to do?"

"I don't know. You're a guy; he's a guy."

"Yes." Jake drew the word out.

"So can't you just go *find* him? Call, leave a message on his machine, and maybe he'll call *you* back if he doesn't want to talk to me. Go to his apartment, and if he doesn't answer the door to you, either, insist that the landlord let you in. The landlord will do it if you demand it. If he *is* in bed with some girlfriend, you can make some hearty male joke and then back out and call me right away. But just, for God's sake, make sure he's not lying in bed with a fever, too sick to answer the door. Make sure he hasn't spent four days throwing up in a pot. If he's not there, leave a note telling him to phone us straightaway. And if he doesn't turn up in twenty-four hours, Jake, I'm calling the police."

She was completely wound up. He wanted to tell her to go work on her pottery wheel, let the clay turn beneath her hands. In the old days, this was when they would have had sex for two hours, when he would have taken that tight spiral of energy and uncoiled it to both their benefits.

"How about if I put in a call to his cell," he said, "and maybe I'll reach him, but if not, we wait one more day?"

"Sunday would be when he would be home, if he's going to be home at all," she said. "He has classes Monday. I think you should go over today. Now. The more I think about it, the more I realize this is the right thing to do, Jake. If you take a cab, it will only take forty-five minutes."

"The gallery's open today," he said.

"Can't one of your girlfriends staff it for an hour?"

Another comment he chose to ignore.

"Jake, please," she said after a minute. "Hang a 'back-in-a-sec' sign. Or I'll catch a cab and come watch the gallery, if you want."

He did think Carol was overreacting. No, he was sure of it. But he wasn't getting any business, anyway. Plus, Jonas was their son even though Carol had done the bulk of the raising. And she didn't ask him for much.

"Okay," he said. "Okay, okay, okay. But Carol, if he is with some young woman, then the next time he doesn't call for nine days, you are just going to have to find a way to be more mellow about it. Agreed?"

"A deal," she said. "Oh, God, let him be with a girl."

Let us all, Jake thought. *Let us all be with a girl.*

Al Zaqr Carpet Shop appeared deserted when Masoud glanced through the picture window from the sidewalk, but as soon as he pushed open the door, Adnan emerged from the tiny back office as he always did, dressed in a light blue *thobe*, stepping gingerly around the thick carpets and carrying a cup the size of a child's fist from which he sipped sweet Turkish coffee. Its aroma mixed with the scent of rug dust in a way that had begun to strike Masoud as cozy. Settled for the past twenty years in his adopted country, Adnan had become as predictable as the call to prayer. His world had narrowed to his shop with its layer upon layer of rugs in shades of deep red and dusty tan, to what he could see from its windows, and to what went on in its two back rooms. He rarely ventured even upstairs to the apartments he rented to fellow Muslims like Masoud. The melancholy that one might expect to result from such an enclosed existence never troubled Adnan—in fact, this lifestyle suited him perfectly. His wife and three daughters bought and prepared his food, friends and neighbors stopped in to share gossip and partake of his generous hospitality, and his six brothers periodically arrived from Lebanon or Saudi Arabia or Iran lugging more carpets for him to sell. Adnan carried a calculator in his pocket and pulled it out as soon as customers entered, promising them a deal. Whether they took him up on it didn't seem to matter much to him, though; he nearly always wore a sweet, contented smile, and he sported the round belly of the satisfied.

"As-salaam aleikum." The two men greeted one another.

"Business is difficult when temperatures dip, isn't that so, brother?" Masoud asked.

"Ah, well." Adnan lifted his chin in a gesture that signaled resignation and contentment at once. "There's business and there is business. It will be better next week, *inshallah*. And if not, then next month."

"So true," Masoud said. "It's in the hands of Allah, glory be upon Him."

"Are you coming to tonight's meeting?" Adnan held monthly father-son meetings in the larger of the back rooms. It gave the Muslim men a sense of community in this foreign land and offered an opportunity for youths to discuss with their elders anything that bothered them. Adnan also had created an informal mentoring system. The meetings were well attended, and Masoud, as a *hajji*, had often been invited to comment on various matters; it had been from the start a useful way for him to make Brooklyn contacts. Sometimes the conversations were basic, centering on matters such as understanding Islam's five pillars, but those

Masoud enjoyed most went deeper to encircle topics of profound knowledge pertaining to the comprehension of sacred mysteries and the ways of Allah, glory be upon Him, and the glorious Qur'an.

"Is the meeting tonight?" Masoud asked now. "I must have confused the date. I'm unavailable tonight."

"Are your plans unbreakable, brother?" Adnan asked. "I hoped to discuss efforts to step up our outreach campaign."

"Ah, yes, your campaign," Masoud said non-committally. Adnan wanted to organize representatives to go into the schools and talk to classes about Islam, how the word itself meant peace, how most of its adherents embraced tolerance.

"It's important work," Adnan countered. "Much is at stake. Those of us who wish to live here—and want our children to share in the opportunities—know it is essential to demonstrate that the extremists among us are few."

"Though we also know *shari'a* permits the use of force under divine guidance to establish justice and equilibrium," Masoud said.

"To understand the Qur'an, Masoud, we must use our hearts, not just our intellects."

"Heart or mind, we must not revoke the foundations of our religion," Masoud pressed.

Adnan cleared his throat. "I understand how difficult it was for your family to suffer a son's loss," he said.

"Ah. Thank you, brother," Masoud said, but he didn't really mean it. He didn't want to discuss his brother, and he doubted Adnan understood. When Masoud's father had called to say Ifraan had been killed in Afghanistan after a rocket attack against the tiny clinic where he had been volunteering, Masoud hadn't believed. He grew furious, called his father a liar. Over the next few days, the United Nations confirmed the rocket attack, but the United States denied it, so Masoud grew convinced that the reports must be wrong. Ifraan was alive, he decided, and hard at work healing patients, completely unaware that his wailing mother mourned his fictional passing. His father tried to dissuade him, but Masoud booked a flight to Kabul, hired a car, and traveled through the dusty, chaotic capital into the rugged, desperate mountains. Even when he saw the hospital rubble with his own eyes, even then, he knelt and began to sift through it, as if he still might find his brother there alive. Some Afghans who lived nearby finally pulled him to his feet, led him away.

"But it is my shared sorrow, brother," Adnan said, grabbing the younger man by his shoulders.

Masoud worked to keep himself from pulling away. He thought about mentioning the case of Abdel Moti Abdel Rahman Mohammad, who'd recently had his left eye surgically removed at King Fahd Hospital in Medina, Saudi Arabia, in a

court-ordered punishment after he had been con-
victed of throwing acid at a man's face, causing
disfigurement and damage to his left eye.
Amnesty International had protested the ruling,
but devout Muslims understood it. He thought
about mentioning to Adnan that he'd never known
the color of his own skin until he'd arrived in this
country, and that men like him—and Adnan—
would never fit in, no matter how many schools
they visited with their messages.

But he said nothing. There was no point.

"At any rate," Adnan added after a moment, "I
remember now that it is you who are right, and I
who am confused. The meeting is tomorrow night.
I hope your prior commitments will allow you to
attend then?"

His tone sounded sincere, but his eyes held the
sly look Masoud had grown to recognize. Adnan
suspected something, and if he could verify his
suspicions, he would likely not hesitate to betray
Masoud—to his family, at least, and perhaps to
American authorities.

"If it's tomorrow night, then I will be there,"
Masoud said, although he wouldn't. "Tonight I
meet with some of our brothers in their homes."

"Yes, of course," Adnan said, his tone mildly
skeptical.

For once, the ringing of his cell phone was a
relief. Masoud looked at the number; it was Bakr.
"Excuse me, brother," he said to Adnan. In the

stairwell, he picked up the phone. *"Salaam aleikum,"* he said.

"Salaam. Abu Asfar al-Amriki left."

Abu Asfar the American: the code name for Jonas. Masoud halted on the stairwell. "What? What do you mean?"

"He's back now."

"In his room?"

"Yes."

"Alone?"

"Yes."

"How long was he gone? Who did he see?"

"No one, I think. I followed him."

"Did he see you? No, wait. Just tell me from the start. What happened?"

"He left the room. He walked down the street and into a shop. He got something to eat. Then he left and walked into another store and bought some things. Then he returned to the apartment."

"He spoke to no one?"

"Not that I saw."

"What did he buy?"

"Hard to tell. Paper, I think. Some tweezers. A few more items."

Masoud took a deep breath. Of the seven who would act tomorrow for Ifraan's revenge, Jonas was the one who worried Masoud most. Jonas was the prize, the blond-haired, Western-raised Wahhabi. *Let's see,* Masoud thought, *if the media will call* him *a terrorist.* Masoud had grown attached to Jonas, drawn to his openness and questioning mind, his ego-less approach to understanding his country. And technically, Jonas had proven himself very able; he'd learned everything they needed during his three weeks of training in Pakistan. Still, he was the least predictable, and thus the most dangerous. If he turned, everything could be ruined. His motivations were complex and personal, in Masoud's view, and a lack of time had prevented the madrassa period that Masoud would have preferred.

Besides, Jonas was born an American. He had family and friends here. Even though he'd rejected his country's ways, these last hours were always tricky. Masoud had spent twelve hours a day with Jonas over this final week, altering his diet and sleep patterns and monitoring his moods, and he was certain Jonas's resolve was strong. Still, when the moment arrived, would Jonas go through with it? Who really knew? His job was to get Jonas to the final step. Allah alone held the eventual outcome in His hands.

Masoud opened the door of his apartment and locked it behind him before speaking. "Okay, Bakr," he said. "Call right away if he leaves again. Right away. And make sure he doesn't make any phone calls."

"That's already been handled," Bakr said.

"Good. I will see you in a few hours."

Masoud sat on his bed to remove his shoes. On

the other side of the room stood a stove, an oven, and a refrigerator. The space was far smaller and more severe than anyplace he'd lived in Riyadh, but he welcomed its asceticism. His prayer rug lay in one corner. His books were piled neatly nearby. Against a wall were seven sets of clean clothes, each stacked individually and topped with seven Qur'ans, ready for delivery tonight.

Masoud went into the bathroom, spread shaving cream on his face, and began to make his cheeks smooth. This would be his second shave of the day, but it was a matter of respect. He wanted to honor the men he would soon be visiting. He wanted the martyrs to know that he both envied them for being chosen and felt humbled before them. The first drop of blood shed by a *shaheed* washes away his sins entirely. And this was the most special of missions for a *shaheed*.

Seven, the holiest of numbers, the most complete. Allah, glory be to Him, ordained seven days in a week and grants seven gifts to his martyrs. Pilgrims on hajj circle seven times around the Ka'ba in Mecca. And so, seven central arteries to the subway. At 9:07 A.M. in New York, on the ninth day of the eleventh month, seven sacred explosions, seven martyrs on their way to the seven heavens. Port Authority. Union Square. Penn Station. Columbus Circle. Times Square. Rockefeller Center. Grand Central. These men were headed for purity. Masoud would remain here, so humanly flawed, but determined to rewrite the significance of his family name and give meaning to his brother's death so that it would not drift into irrelevance. Ifraan deserved that.

Masoud took three swipes with the razor, and then the cell phone, which he'd set on the toilet seat, rang again. He flipped it open to see that the call came from overseas. His father's cell phone. He glanced at his watch, which he kept set to the time in Mecca. His father was calling when his father should be sleeping. He hesitated, then quickly wiped the cream off his left cheek. He held the phone to his ear.

"*As-salaam*, Father."

"Masoud, where are you?" His father's voice sounded sharp across the many miles. This was a man who played in three chords: flirtatious when speaking to attractive Western women, obsequious when talking to his social betters in Riyadh, and dictatorial when addressing the family.

"You know where I am. I am in New York."

"Masoud." The line crackled, possibly a sign that they were being overheard but maybe simply due to the distance between the two phones. "Masoud, I have been hearing things that do not please me."

Masoud glanced at his reflection in the mirror, wiping away a little of the cream near the inside of his left eyebrow. "What things, Father?"

"I am not going into detail over these cursed phones," his father said. "Twenty-two men in suits may be listening as we speak. But if there's any truth to it, you should know that I'm hearing it here. And if I'm hearing it here, it is being heard across all the world's deserts and in all the cities and in Mecca itself. So if you were counting on secrecy for unforgivable, anti-Islamic acts—"

That rumors were circulating was very unwelcome news, but he didn't want his father to hear any concern in his voice. His father would read it, rightly, as confirmation. "I'm surprised you got through, Father," he said, sitting on the edge of the bathtub. "My phone has been failing me lately. I don't know how long the connection will last."

"Islam is a religion of moderation and morality. You are interpreting *shari'a* to fit your private purposes, and that is a sin. Your understanding of duty to family and religion is, at best, erroneous."

It is you, Father, who have misunderstood your duty and left it to me to rescue our name. Aloud, Masoud said only, "I wish it were easier, Father, to make out your words."

His father sighed. "We lost Ifraan. You think I don't feel it as his father? But there are other ways, more restrained ways—"

Masoud interrupted. "How is my mother?"

"Yes," said Masoud's father. "Think of your mother. She barely survived your brother. Do not, Masoud, do not—"

"Father," Masoud interrupted, "forgive me. Your voice is so fragmented I cannot make out the meaning."

"I want this conversation in person. I insist that you return home now, with your hands unsullied, Masoud."

"*Inshallah*, Father." Easy enough for Masoud to agree. After all, the private jet with its private pilot and its access to a private tarmac—it had all already been arranged, though his father didn't yet know that.

"You do not have the right to make choices for us all," his father was continuing. "Make no mistake, what you do affects your sisters, your mother and me, my relations with the king and—"

"The line, Father. It is so poor."

"I said my relations with—"

Masoud pressed the end button, hanging up the phone. "My relations with my yachts," he muttered to himself.

He'd maintained a respectful attitude toward his father, but that was the extent of what he could take for today. He needed quiet to think about these intercontinental rumors. He didn't want to change his plans, nor did he want to see them disrupted through premature revelations. He had to focus now, stay attentive to every detail if he were to make the right choices. He had taken on a historic assignment, and he needed to reflect with courage and calm. Allah, glory be upon Him, had set Masoud on a path to give meaning to his brother's death, and Allah, glory be upon Him, would guide him now. Masoud inhaled deeply, calming himself, and continued to slide the razor's blade over his face.

NEW YORK: 5:40 P.M.
MECCA: 1:40 A.M.

Sonny felt like dancing. He'd been raking it in. He hadn't counted yet, and wouldn't until he was alone, but he expected this would add up to the best day of the season so far, and for sure he'd done better than most any business aboveground. It was purely glacial on the street, without even snow to make it glistening and beautiful. No reason to linger upstairs. So everyone was diving into the subway, and when they saw Sonny moving their way with the slow, purposeful shuffle he'd perfected over the years, they started feeling guilty. His eyes were clear and his voice gentle and he knew he reminded folk—even white folk—of their own grandfathers. Who, on a cold day like this, could stand to see his grandfather without enough change to buy a hot bowl of soup? It didn't hurt, either, that it was a Sunday. People mostly weren't headed into the office, so they weren't knotted up inside about how hard they had to work and how tired they were of their jobs and how they hated their bosses and how, on top of that, Sonny—luxuriating in the ranks of the unemployed—was wanting a piece of their salaries just for the asking.

He expected tomorrow to be a rippin' day, too. After all, it would be just as cold. Now, though, it was starting to get dark, and he was bone-tired. He decided to head toward his sister's, even though he might get another good hour out of the subway. The beauty of being self-employed: he could clock out when he wanted. He needed to leave his day's take with Ruby, and he needed to be clean and fresh for Monday morning. He would shower and then visit a bit, since it wasn't polite to just wash and run, as he liked to joke with Ruby.

When he came aboveground, he saw that the heavy clouds had made the street darker than it should be this early. He tightened his hold on his earnings. He carried the money in a worn knapsack someone had thrown away in a trash can at the 42nd Street Port Authority station, and now he tucked the knapsack under his coat. Folks knew him around his sister's place; they might guess he was coming with some coins at the end of a day, and he didn't want some junkie to jump him. The cops seemed to all be underground today, keeping warm, worrying about something that would probably never come to pass, leaving devils to harass folks up above.

His cheeks stung from the cold and then went numb as the wind screamed shrilly on its way down the tunnel of the street that emptied into the Hudson. The gale was at his back, at least, so it pushed him quickly toward Ruby's. Between the station and Ruby's, he saw only three men outside, warming their hands over a fire burning in an oil drum in front of Henry's Restaurant Equipment and Supply Corp. A second later, he was at his destination. He pressed the bell, and Ruby's voice came fast, as if she'd been waiting. "Who's there?"

"Sonny." He yelled to be heard above the wind. The door buzzed to signal that she'd unlocked it. He shoved it open and headed up the three flights and there she stood, waiting at the entrance to the apartment. "Get in here," she said, wrapping him in a quick embrace and stepping back to pull him inside.

She held on to him for a long minute and then released him and stroked his cheek. He immediately felt the comfort of the indoor air. She held his cold hands between hers and rubbed them. "Sonny," she said, "I knew it. I knew you'd come today."

Sonny wasn't sure what that meant, but he just grinned. "Well, here I be," he said.

He saw Leo then, standing stiffly at the door to the kitchen. Leo was staring at Sonny's shoes, though Sonny couldn't guess why because they weren't too bad—dirty, of course, but shoes were allowed to be. A little torn on the right insole, but otherwise just like new-from-the-store to Sonny's eyes. A junkie had sold them to him for two dollars a week ago, though Sonny wouldn't be telling Leo that. Ruby glanced back at Leo, and under her gaze, he attempted to smile at Sonny, but it more closely resembled a grimace.

"How's business, Leo?" Sonny asked.

"Business is good, Sonny. Seems everybody's in the mood to buy homes this month."

Sonny nodded. He wanted to dislike Leo, but under the circumstances, he couldn't. "You sure taking good care of my sister, Leo," he said.

Ruby pulled Sonny's arm. "You're just in time for some dinner."

Sonny followed Ruby into the kitchen. The dishwasher was open and partly full, the table mostly cleared. "Looks like you already ate here, Ruby," Sonny said.

She reached to a shelf above her head to get a bowl. "Plenty waiting for you. I made Sunday beef stew, just like Momma used to make."

"Hmm." He nodded appreciatively. He shrugged out of his coat and set it on the chair next to him. Ruby was not the cook their momma had been. Still, it smelled good, and this was a pretty fancy meal for Ruby. Must have taken her some time.

She put a bowl before him. "Eat," she said. She brought him two pieces of bread and grated some fresh ginger into a pot and added water and set it to boil. She didn't talk much, but every now and then, she came over to squeeze his arm. She went to the cupboard and pulled out three candles and lit them, placing them carefully in the middle of the kitchen table. Then she sat down beside him. "So you remembered today," she said.

"Today," he said speculatively, noncommittally, staring deep into the stew in the bowl.

"It's the anniversary." Her voice was soft and expectant.

"Well, ain't that right," he said, her words jarring his memory. "Ain't that right." So that was why the candles and the stew. He reached out and patted her hand.

She rose abruptly. "I was looking through the old album," she said. She disappeared for a moment and returned with a large, worn, dark-brown picture album. She opened it on the table in front of them. "Look. The three of us."

Sonny leaned forward and peered. A posed black-and-white snapshot: Sonny and Ruby in front, their mother behind. Momma wore a dark, smooth-fitting dress and that silver cross of hers around her neck, while Ruby, still slightly taller than Sonny in those days, wore a short-sleeved dress that sprang out from her waist. Sonny had on a miniature suit. He would never have recognized himself. Ruby's shy grin was pretty much the same, but otherwise she, too, was completely changed. Momma, though, looked just like Sonny always remembered her: lined forehead, smiling mouth, shoulders back. She always told Ruby and Sonny to carry themselves straight because once they started to bend over with their troubles, that was good as giving up; that meant the troubles were halfway to winning.

"This," Sonny said, "is how we can know there's an afterlife, just like Momma always said."

Ruby tipped her head. "How do you mean?"

"Well, that little boy." Sonny tapped his right pointer-finger on the tiny image of himself. "He dead. He don't exist anymore. But me, I'm still here. Touch me. Go on." Ruby laughed a little and squeezed Sonny's arm. "So that's what it's like when we be dying, Ruby. Momma still exists, just she somewhere else right now."

Ruby shook her head, a sad smile tugging at her lips. "Don't know what I'd do without you, Sonny. You always do make me feel better."

"She probably in the expanse of Heaven right now, kicking up her feet dancing," Sonny said, warming to his subject. "Or belting some rambunctious boy."

"Oh, Sonny." Ruby poked his arm. "She never belted you."

"The hell she didn't."

"If she did, you deserved it. You were wild in those days." Ruby flipped a couple of pages and pointed to another picture of Sonny, about fifteen, clowning for the camera with a stern, forbidding expression. "Can't you just see the mischief in that face?"

"Mischief" was a nice word for it. Both of them knew, after all, that crack had played a part in Sonny's life turning out like it had, and crack surely qualified as more than mischief, though he'd never become a full-out addict and finally lost interest; turned out lucky that way.

This picture Sonny only glanced at, not really interested in a long look. He took another spoonful of the stew. What he remembered from those teenaged years was how narrow the world seemed, how limited to whatever block he and Ruby and Momma were living on, to the hard, thick walls of the neighborhood school, and to the friends who lived nearby and were as dissatisfied as he. There were three who didn't make it, and another four or five who ended up in jail, but the rest were probably still trapped on those blocks, still fighting a dissatisfaction they were trying to ignore. Some of the old apartment buildings were close enough that he could walk there if he had to. But to his way of thinking, he'd ridden that subway right out of his hometown—even if it was just to another part of New York—and made good. Or good enough.

"You hold on to these memories, Ruby," he said, " 'cause you do it for all of us."

He took one more sip of stew, wiped his mouth with the napkin Ruby had set before him, and reached into his coat to pull out the bag holding his day's earnings. He dumped it on the kitchen table, and Ruby pushed aside the photo album and began helping him separate the coins from the bills, and then the quarters from the dimes, and so on. Leo came to stand at the door of the kitchen, watching as though he expected them to do a magic trick.

"Two hundred sixty-four dollars and thirty cents," Ruby said when they finished. "Lordy, Sonny. That's a good day's work."

Leo snorted, but they both ignored him.

"Put it with the rest, now," Sonny said.

Ruby tilted her head and looked at him, silent for a moment. Then she stood up and poured him a cup of the ginger tea that she always insisted he drink. She thought it protected him from infection. And truth was, despite the subway drafts and the viruses carried by commuters and other subway dwellers, he couldn't remember last time he'd gotten sick. Ruby placed the tea before him, sat and leaned over the table. "Sonny," she said, "you got quite a pile now. When are you going to use it to come in off the street?"

"Now, there's the question," said Leo, who hadn't moved from the kitchen door.

Ruby ignored her husband. "Momma would like it to see you somewhere regular for the nights, somewhere warm-like," she said.

"The irony never ceases to amaze me: I sell houses, and you're homeless," Leo said.

Ruby shot him a look over her shoulder but remained concentrated on Sonny, waiting for him to speak.

Sonny took a sip of the spicy tea before answering. Ruby made it strong, and it lit up his

143

throat on the way down. "We already been down this crooked road, Ruby," he said.

"I know, and I sat quiet on the question for a long time, but tonight, I gotta ask again, Sonny."

Sonny thought back, must have been eight or ten years ago, when Ruby had insisted he see a head doctor, set up an appointment, and walked him to the office. She thought then that with a little mental health counseling, Sonny would choose to change his profession and lifestyle. He felt uncomfortable as soon as he stepped into that starchy office, but he walked up to the receptionist and announced, "I be doing this for Ruby."

"Name, please," the receptionist said.

"Sonny Hirt." The receptionist, with a mole on right cheek and fingernails painted with a checked design, looked familiar. "I may know you," he said. "You ever seen me on the subway?"

She glanced at him coolly. "Take a seat, Mr. Hirt. It'll be a few minutes."

He did sit then. He sat for about ten minutes, until that doctor's waiting room began to feel like the principal's office and he couldn't stay anymore. Then he just walked out. He waited six months to go see Ruby again, to press home his point that she had to take him as he was.

"I got myself a home, Ruby," Sonny said now. "Biggest home imaginable. Stretching through all five boroughs. I got places to sit and a bed comfortable enough, and . . . and I entertain a lot. . . ." He guffawed.

"If you got yourself a home, then why do you come here to shower?" Leo asked.

Ruby straightened up and turned fully toward her husband. "Leo," she said, and there was a stripe of iron in her voice, "this is the anniversary of my momma's death. Sonny and I are going to spend some time talking now. You're welcome to sit with us, but you might be more comfortable seeing what's on TV, the way you usually do."

Leo shifted his weight without answering at first. "Guess you're right," he finally said.

She watched him leave and then turned back to Sonny. He saw more of Momma in her worn expression than he ever had before. "You know, I was sitting here looking at these pictures, all the way from when we were babies, Sonny, and seeing all the love in Momma's face. You can see how proud she is. And then I wonder, what went wrong? What went wrong, Sonny?"

Sonny looked directly at her eyes, which were starting to fill, and he had to stop that or Leo might run in here and accuse Sonny of making his wife cry. It had happened like that before.

"Nothin' wrong," he said, though he knew that wasn't enough to put an end to it.

"Oh, Sonny." Ruby stroked the top of the kitchen table with her palm. "No matter how I've tried to change it, you're living on the streets, and you know that would upset Momma. And me, I got a home and I got Leo, but . . . but it wasn't what I was expecting."

Sonny ran his finger around the rim of his cup. "I know you be holding these questions tight in your head—they're good questions, Ruby, about the course of life and all," he said. "But you got to remember. You got an everyday man. That's something Momma didn't have. And you got yourself what else we never did, when we were little. These walls around you that you can count on. That ain't nothing, so with all your worrying, don't forget that. Remember all those times we had to be moving, a block over or to the end of the street, trying to make it in places that each one be feeling smaller and dirtier than the one before? Momma was always struggling. She'd be pleased and proud to see you not struggling, Ruby."

"Not that way, at least," she said.

"Not that way," he agreed. He took another sip of her tea and then went on, "And about me, well, I'm the happiest guy in the world."

She laughed. "In the *world,* is it?"

"I got somethin' to judge that by, too, Ruby, 'cause every day I see hundreds of people. You know how it is with me: I can walk into a place and feel a body. I walk in here and feel you wanting for more with Leo, for instance. With them folks brushing by me, or reaching to put a coin in my hand, I'm feeling some of the same.

They all be longing for something. A steady diet of longing, Ruby, well, that drives a person to the needle or the gun. Me, looks like from the outside I got less, but I'm not *longing* for more, and there's a freedom in that. I don't know why, and I'm not trying to brag on it. But I'm free in a way Momma never was, and I think she'd be full glad for it. For me, it's still a plenty good life."

"Listen to you," Ruby said, and her face was a bit lighter now, as if her cheekbones had risen half an inch and the skin beneath them had magically tightened. "Talking the way you do, like a subway philosopher." She reached out to tug playfully on his right ear. "You know, you could have gotten married, quite a few times."

He grinned at her. "You saying it's too late now?"

Ruby laughed. "Lord, no. We clean you up a bit, maybe a blue silk tie, and you're still a catch." Then she gestured out the kitchen window. "Stay here tonight at least. It's bitter cold out there."

He glanced toward the kitchen door, which led to the living room and its sound of the television's canned laughter. Ruby followed his gaze.

"Oh, him," she said. "He don't understand, Sonny. Don't let him worry you."

For a moment, Sonny considered spending the night on Ruby's couch, resting his head on a real pillow. He'd taken her up on the offer a few times over the years. The night he got rolled in the

Times Square station, for instance. They sliced his neck near the jawline, yanked back his arm, and bloodied his eye for the love of about twenty-two bucks. He made it to Ruby's and spent close to a week on her couch. He was certainly thankful for Ruby. But tonight he felt loaded with optimism and ready to go.

"Leaving my earnings with you, Ruby, it's saving me a pile of worry," he said, "and I'm thinking I'll likely be back with more tomorrow night, because tomorrow's going to be another good day for Mr. Sonny. I feel it. But now I'm thinking, with your blessing, I'll just be getting a shower and shoving on."

Ruby looked down at her hands and straightened her fingers as if studying her nails. "Even though it's Momma's anniversary?" she asked.

"Even so."

She shook her head, but when she met his gaze, she was smiling softly. "You're a hardheaded man," she said. "I'll go get you a fresh towel." At the kitchen door, she turned back to him. "Thank you, Sonny," she said. "For coming tonight. Wouldn't have been the same without you."

"Ruby," he said, full of tenderness. There weren't many around to praise Sonny for meeting family obligations. He clenched his fist lightly, kissed the top of it, and blew it in the direction of his sister.

NEW YORK: 6:25 P.M.
MECCA: 2:25 A.M.

Jake had been consumed by trying to figure out exactly how to present the facts to Carol so she wouldn't get too upset and they could logically discuss what to do next, and because of this he hadn't given a thought to what it might feel like to be standing outside his old building until he was there. It was odd that in all this time, she'd never moved and even odder to think that he could have continued coming here every evening after work forever. In that case, this would just be an evening like any other instead of an evening that marked the first time he'd been here in, what? Fifteen years? In this other, no-divorce reality, they might be upstairs watching the news together, having already talked through what to do about Jonas, or they might be bumping hips in the kitchen, making a cheese-and-mushroom omelet to share.

Probably romanticized visions, all, but how could he be anything but romantic standing in front of the building that had contained him during the most hopeful days of his life? The name over the buzzer still combined hers and his. Carol Meitzner. She'd never changed it back to her maiden name, and that moved him in a way that he suspected it probably should not. She would say even noticing was a sign of his self-involvement, but she was still the only woman he'd ever given his name to—or ever would, he suspected now—and he had to admit he felt pleased that she'd kept it. He thought about ringing the buzzer in their code pattern: three short and one long. That game had enabled them to skip the step of pressing the intercom button and calling, "Yes?" Before Jonas, it allowed one to greet the other naked, if they wanted, because the unspoken rule was that you used the code only if you were coming up alone.

But if he used the code, she might discover how tightly he still clung to old dreams, and consider him pathetic. Or *he* might discover she'd forgotten it, which would feel—just wrong.

Whatever. It was too cold to be out here musing, so he leaned on the buzzer, waited a second, and then gave it a last short tap for good measure.

"Hello?"

"It's me," Jake said, and she buzzed him in.

It remained a nice building, well maintained, he noticed as he got into the elevator and pushed the button for the eleventh floor. The aroma of spaghetti sauce clung to the elevator just as it had when he'd lived here.

She was waiting for him in the hallway when the elevator door opened. Still slender, with hair that hung to her shoulders. He took in these details even though he knew what she looked like—Jonas showed him photographs every so often.

"I kept thinking you'd call," she said. "Was he there?"

"No. Can I come in?"

She waved her hand.

Inside the door, he pulled off his coat and dropped it on a tan leather easy chair he'd never seen before. She had the same bookcase, but otherwise, everything was different, including the artwork on the wall. One was a photograph of a woman in a green dress flying an orange kite. Another was a terracotta-colored painting of a form that looked vaguely like Buddha. He walked into the kitchen and reached up into the cabinet where they used to keep the coffee cups. They were still there. He took down a cup he recognized, off-white with a lavender flower painted on the side.

"Can I help you to something?" she said pointedly.

"Well, if you still keep the tea over there," he said, pointing to the narrow, built-in cabinet, "I can probably help myself."

"That may be more familiarity than I want." She opened the cabinet he'd pointed to and pulled out three boxes—Earl Gray, green, and chamomile—for him to choose from. She set them on the kitchen table. He filled his cup with water and put it in the microwave. In the corner of the countertop, she still had the metal teapot they used to take with them when they went camping. She had stuck some dried flowers in it.

She followed his gaze but didn't comment on the teapot. "Okay, Jake. What did you find out?"

"There was no answer on any of his phones or at the door," he said. "I buzzed the landlord's apartment, and there was no answer there, either. Finally I found someone in the damn building, a girl who is a personal trainer and knows Jonas, at least a little bit. We talked for a while until she was convinced I was okay and really Jonas's dad, and then she told me the landlord was at his brother's house on East 8th, helping fix up an apartment. She didn't know exactly where, but she said the corner of 8th and 63rd, so I went there and rang a few bells, God, it was cold—"

"Jake," she said. "Jonas. This is about Jonas."

"Yeah. I found the guy, finally. He didn't want to stop what he was doing to go let me into Jonas's apartment, but he finally agreed to send his nephew with me and—" He broke off. This was where it would start to get tricky, he knew, so he took the cup out of the microwave and added a bag of green tea.

"Go ahead," Carol said.

"Let's go sit in the living room," Jake said.

"Does this really have to be orchestrated?" Carol asked, but she followed him into the living room. He noticed she took the chair across from the couch so there was no chance he could sit close enough to touch her.

"So he let me in," he said, sitting on the couch.

"And the room was neat—very neat, actually, for Jonas. The bed was made and all the clothes were put away and the dishes clean. It looked like he'd gotten ready for company—or maybe just for a visit from you." He smiled and took a sip of tea.

"So it didn't look like he'd been there?"

"The room smelled kind of stale, so I think maybe he hadn't been there in a couple days, but that's only a guess." He set down his tea and leaned back. "My best bet remains that he's found himself a new girlfriend who lives in a nicer apartment than his."

"I want to call the police," Carol said.

"Wait a minute." Jake held up one hand. "There's a little more. I looked around some. I searched on his desk and found a few things. First of all, paperwork from NYU. He's not enrolled this semester, Carol. I guess he was too late filling out some forms?"

"What? What's he been doing all day, then? And why did he lie to me?"

"They said he could enroll next semester, so we'll make sure he follows through. The part that bothered me, though, Carol," and here he paused again, "is that neither of you told me he went to Pakistan."

Carol shook her head. "What are you talking about?"

"I found a ticket stub for a flight to Pakistan."

"What?"

Jake felt a tightening in his chest. He'd hoped that he'd simply been left out of the loop. The thought that Jonas had gone somewhere like Pakistan without mentioning it to either parent made him distinctly uneasy.

"In early September," he said. "Something like the second or the third."

"Pakistan?" she said. "He told me he was going on a yoga retreat in Vermont before school started. He even sent me an e-mail describing the weather and the food."

"I don't know, Carol." Jake shook his head. "E-mails can come from anywhere. There's a used airline ticket on the corner of his desk that says Jonas Meitzner flew into Islamabad and then flew out three weeks later.

Carol stood up. She walked around the room, rubbing her arms.

"There is also a train ticket stub. The Abaseen Railcar, it said in English. Took Jonas to Peshawar."

"Peshawar?"

"It's near the border," Jake said. "Maybe he was touring around?"

Carol held her hand over her mouth for a moment, as though holding in a scream, and then took it away.

"One more thing," Jake said. "I left the tickets, but this I brought with me." He stood up and reached for his jacket. He pulled a piece of printer paper from the inside pocket and handed it to her.

She unfolded it as she sat on the edge of the couch.

Jake stood over her shoulder, looking at the page that had Arabic writing in the lower left-hand corner and a sketch in the center that looked like steps leading to a box, with more boxes inside. "I don't know what the drawing is supposed to show, but isn't this Jonas's handwriting?" he said, pointing to the words underneath. One line read, "Islamabad. Sadabaha bus stand." The other line, underlined twice, read, "3rd car, 3rd door, 3rd stop."

"We've got to find him," Carol said. She was starting to hyperventilate.

"Look," Jake said. "Let's just slow down. Maybe he just didn't mention this to us because he thought we would worry about him going to Islamabad, or Lahore, or Peshawar, whatever. And maybe we would have if we'd known. Maybe he just didn't want to deal with the old folks on this one. So let's go through what you *do* know, what he *has* told you. Maybe the girlfriend is Pakistani?"

"I think he's confused, Jake," Carol said. "I think he's in some kind of trouble."

"What about friends? Anybody from Pakistan? Or *near* Pakistan?"

Carol leaned forward. "No, not Pakistan," she said. "But let me think, let me think." She put one hand on her forehead. "This is what I remember. Last spring he was taking some kind of comparative religion class at some organization on the Upper West Side. SAWU—the Society for the Advancement of World Understanding. I think that's it. Something grandiose and all-encompassing like that. And he told me that in the class, he met this really interesting man. Mohammed, or Mahmoud, or, no, that's not it exactly. He was impressed with the guy. I think he came from some upper-class Saudi family or something. Jonas said he was very clear and moral. This is part of this stage he's been going through. You know, where he labels everything moral or immoral, even though he says that's, I don't know, simplistic." She took a deep breath, biting her thumbnail, and then shook her head. "That's it. He liked the guy, and then he never mentioned him again, and I don't know anything else."

"Okay," Jake said. "Good. So let's look up this Society for the Advancement of whatever on the web, and in the morning we'll call and see if they have a student list from last spring, and we'll try to get in touch with this Mohammed."

"It's not Mohammed," Carol said. "And are you thinking we aren't going to be able to get in touch with Jonas, then?"

"Look, if Jonas went to Pakistan without telling us, maybe he's—I don't know, Carol—maybe he's traveling somewhere else right now?"

Carol groaned in frustration. "Goddamn it, Jake. If he just took off without saying anything . . ."

"Carol, every parent in the history of parenthood has had to deal with something like this, some kid who just flat failed to take into account the amount of worry he was going to cause his parents. We've been pretty damn lucky up until now. Maybe this is our turn. And remember, he's not fifteen. He's twenty-one. He's solid. He's reasonable. He's responsible—"

"Not too damn responsible," she said.

He sighed. "That's our boy."

She gave a strange, weak laugh, and her shoulders seemed to loosen just a little. "I've been so worried, Jake, and I didn't know what to do and—" She broke off, waved her hand. "This one's . . ." she said. "I can't do this one alone."

He took her shoulders and pulled her close, surprised that she allowed it.

"You want me to stay tonight?" he said. "Sleep on the couch. Just be here, with you. And tomorrow we'll start first thing; we'll just work this until we track him down."

She sighed and reached to the back of her neck, beginning to rub. He wished he could do it for her, but he knew if he tried, she'd send him right to the door. "You know," she said after a minute, and then she hesitated before going on. "You know, that might be nice, Jake."

He smiled. "You got an extra toothbrush?" he asked. "Or should I go to the corner to pick one up?"

NEW YORK: 7:18 P.M.
MECCA: 3:18 A.M.

By the time he heard tapping at his door, Jonas was eating Saltines, carelessly letting the golden crumbs scatter on his chest as he reviewed what he'd already accomplished.

Trim and file nails, toes and fingers both.

Now only the narrowest moon-sliver of ivory rose above the pink core of his nails married to his flesh. He photographed his trimmed feet against the red chenille bedspread and unexpectedly realized he had attractive feet. He wasn't sure he'd ever paid full attention to them before. He wondered what it might have been like to have been a foot model, if he—or his feet—would have had what it took. The right look. He wondered if such a job actually existed, where one simply had to show up and allow one's feet to be photographed on golden beaches or dipping into pools of water or resting on rose-colored petals ripped from flowers. He imagined the photographs as part of advertisements for hotels or spas or airlines. He wondered if America had become so distorted that a foot model might be paid thousands for a day's work while a middle school teacher took a second job driving taxis at night to feed his children. Then he decided not to muddy his thoughts with political analysis or even rants—he'd already done that, and he'd already made his decision. Instead he would simply appreciate his shapely feet. He wondered how he had gotten them. Not from his mother—he remembered unattractive bunions and a crooked third toe on the right foot. He couldn't recall his father's feet with any specificity.

Shave hair around genitals.

He'd been putting that off for as long as he could, initially justifying the delay by the need for fresh razors. Even after buying the extra razors, though, he'd waited. This, after all, would be different from shaving the rest of his body. Finally he forced himself into the bathroom, where he trimmed the hair close, used a washcloth to warm the skin, and then applied the shaving cream. He drew a deep breath before swiping carefully in the direction that his hair grew. It took four runs over the same vulnerable territory before a pale highway of flesh made its way through his second chakra of sensuality and pleasure. He kept going, feeling as if he were shaving off chapters of his life, traveling backward in time, out of reach of Vic, out of reach of adulthood, even. Back to some imagined boyhood when his view of the world was shaped solely by others. A burial: that was what it felt like. A farewell to Jonas the young man, to what he'd already experienced, and what he never would.

Afterward, he took his cell phone from under his bed pillow, a longing to call Vic moving through his body. He cupped the phone in his hand as though holding it could stave off his desire. The phone was contraband. He wasn't supposed to have it. He was permitted contact with no one in these remaining hours. He needed to purify and pray and concentrate, not be tempted by distractions from the very world he hoped to sanitize through his actions.

Still, there was Vic. How could he but be distracted by her? It had been not quite three months since it had begun between them on Long Horn Lake, but the attraction had been building in him for two years, maybe more. In late August, as summer began to slip away and just a couple of weeks before he went to Pakistan, he and Vic went together to the Adirondacks. He was becoming immersed in Islam, but not so much that he would sacrifice his friendship with Vic. Still, he knew better than to mention to Masoud that they were going camping together. That would be *haram*, forbidden.

Long Horn was framed by skyscraper pines and compact honey maples turning golden before their time, and they found a spot where they could tamp down the wispy grass, pitch a tent, and hear the water speak. They had a map; in the morning, they planned to hike a seven-mile trail up through the woods to a six-foot waterfall and a flat-topped rock that jutted from the earth, a type of rock locals called a glacial retort. They joked about its name and recalled, still laughing, glacial retorts they had given or received.

They'd gone camping together before, over the years. Jonas, considering it as he packed for the trip, decided it was strange that they'd managed to share a tent six or eight times without a bit of sexual tension rearing its head. Then he admitted to himself that wasn't quite true. He'd felt sexual tension, but he'd pushed it away, reminding himself that Vic was like a sister. Now, suddenly, his repressed desires bobbed to the surface. Close as he and Vic were after their years of friendship, he wanted more intimacy. She was smart and driven in all the right ways. And beautiful. And lithe. Though he vowed not to act upon his cravings, he credited Masoud for helping him identify the way Vic made him feel. Clarity in the spiritual sphere, it seemed, led to clarity in the earthly realm as well.

Every time they camped, Vic awoke first in the morning and started right up, stoking the fire, making tea, calling to Jonas, "Up, up, you can sleep when you're dead, boy." Vic always had high energy, but the wilderness seemed to give her even more. On that late-August trip, however, a rain no one had forecast began in the night. In the morning, when she poked her head out of the tent, he said, half-asleep, "C'mon, Vic. It's way too wet out there."

She flung herself back, clearly disappointed. "What are we going to do, then?" That question hung in the air for a moment, taunting them. Still wordless, they both reached out, as if into air, as if any contact would be a mistake, and then they touched one another, nothing more than a graze, and something was unleashed.

It rained for four more precious hours. When it stopped, the sky turned a firm blue, its color absorbed by the lake, and the pine needles glistened. The place where they'd pitched the tent looked changed, magical.

Afterward Jonas wondered if it had only been a particular mood that had seized Vic, trapped as she was in a tent during a storm. He worried the question for a few days and then he asked. Perhaps she regretted it? Perhaps it was too trivial to even regret? "God, Jonas," she said. And she pressed her body close to his, as close as she could get, and leaned her head away, arching her back but still watching him, and then she took his head in her hands and pulled him toward her and he felt like part of a dance she was choreographing on the spot except that she shuddered slightly, involuntarily, and she said it again, only a little slower, a little softer. "God. Jonas."

By now, though, at least ten days had gone by since Vic had called, and he knew what that meant. He didn't blame her. He was a pain. Moody and intense. Sometimes worry gave him stomachaches. Sometimes his thoughts raced so fast he could barely hang on to them.

Sitting in the apartment on the Avenue of the Finest, Jonas wished for and imagined three or four different versions of a conversation he longed to have with her before tomorrow. He pictured himself saying, "Thank you, Vic. I love you, Vic. I love your laugh, and I love the way you touch your upper lip with your tongue sometimes, and how you pull on your ear when you are thinking. I love the time we shared, even though you ended it. So thank you." He'd never spoken like that to her before, with all walls knocked down, but he thought he would like to. If he called, he wondered whether she might laugh at his speech and say, "Please come spend one last night with me." He would take that night, if he could. Then he thought about her show, which opened in a couple of days twenty-three blocks from where he now sat, and then he didn't want to think about her anymore.

Still holding the cell phone, he considered calling his mother. He'd been keeping his distance lately, both because Masoud kept him busy and because Masoud insisted Jonas curb ties with his "old life." Jonas missed his mother's laugh, the way she always smelled like earth from the pots she threw. His mother had rapid-fire intuitions when it came to Jonas, though. He suspected just the tone of his voice would worry her, and he didn't want that. She'd probably trace the call and show up at the doorstep of this odd little apartment on the Avenue of the Finest—a thought that made him smile. Until fourth grade, he'd believed that after his mother dropped him off at school, she spent the hours lingering outside, occasionally peeking in the window, waiting for the dismissal bell.

He supposed all kids had trouble imagining their parents' lives unbound from their own. Jonas's mother made it particularly hard because she was so centered on him. She made and sold ceramic dishes and mugs and threw those curvy pots of brilliant colors and irregularly shaped openings that were on occasion displayed in art shows. She was the artist, actually, while not a part of the art scene that included Jonas's father. She did her pottery work at night, after Jonas slept, in a designated "mud room" off the kitchen. For years while he was in school, she held down a job keeping books for a chiropractor in his office four blocks from their home. She never much liked it, but the hours were flexible; she always had time for her son. After he moved out to start college, she quit. Still, Jonas's room remained, neater than when he'd lived there but otherwise the same, as if waiting for his return. His mother, a lively, vivid woman still, clearly needed to rework the threads of her life and didn't know how. Jonas suspected that desire for something new and fuller lay buried deep within her like an unborn seed. He felt convinced she wouldn't pursue this desire until he was gone in a more definitive way. As painful as it would be for her, he predicted his absence would force her to renew her own life. The maturity of that thought cheered him in a self-congratulatory way.

He put the cell phone back under his pillow then, removed his jeans, and set himself up under the table lamp next to his bed, placing one leg and then the other under its diffuse yellow light.

Use tweezers to remove stray hairs missed in shaving.

He only did this for a short while because he discovered that pulling hair with tweezers hurts a lot, and besides, it was kind of obsessive behavior. He tugged his jeans back on.

Then he flipped through the magazine he'd bought. The cover showed a grinning man in reflective glasses skiing during a snowfall, the photograph so vivid Jonas could imagine airy flakes the size of cotton balls falling into his mouth. The cold, sweet taste of them. The excitement of the speed, cutting through virgin snow. The articles had titles that began with phrases like "Survival Guide" and "Tricks and Tips." Jonas studied an advertisement for a particular brand of skis he'd once tried on. Then he ripped out an artsy photograph of a run crisscrossed with ski prints and inhabited by one lonely skier in red casting a narrow shadow. He taped it to the wall.

Jonas loved to ski. His father had taught him

years ago, when he'd been a boy. Those skiing lessons may have been the closest he'd ever felt to his dad, and probably the reason he initially loved the sport so much. Separated from his mother, his father was an odd parent: jovial, friendly, but only mildly interested in his son. Jonas couldn't remember his father ever disciplining him. There'd been something unexpectedly nurturing about the times they'd skied together. Once Jonas's father had placed Jonas's skis inside his own and together they'd slalomed down the hill, a strange four-legged creature leaning from side to side simultaneously, and he'd felt safe.

After thinking about the time with his father, Jonas prayed. He pulled a frankincense incense stick from a pocket in his backpack, lit it, and stuck it in a ceramic holder he'd also brought. He photographed the incense several times, trying to capture the thin smoke-needle floating upward. He fingered his prayer beads and recited the hundred names of Allah, which he'd memorized over two days back in July. Then he bowed his head to the floor and presented himself, murmuring partial prayers: "O Great, O Merciful, all thanks . . . your will." The words felt, even to him, a bit perfunctory. Masoud encouraged him to face toward Mecca and chant prayers five times per day, but Mecca, Jonas had decided, was not a city near the Red Seacoast but a state of mind, and he was more likely to reach it if his prayer was as spontaneous as possible and called upon a mix of traditions: Islam, his father's Judaism, the Catholicism he'd been exposed to by a childhood friend, the Buddhism he'd studied briefly. If he were lucky, as he prayed, an image occurred to him, or he felt supported, or tugged in a certain direction. This time he felt nothing. He listened to the call to prayer on his iPod and tried again. He felt nothing still, but he refused to let that worry him.

He thought again of calling Vic. Instead he decided to lie back on the bed to try to locate the tension in his body and release it. Jonas's body tended to run cold; he normally needed extra blankets and several layers under his jackets, but now, though temperatures were low outside, he felt warm, almost like he was sweating beneath his skin, at the skeletal level. He lay on top of the red chenille bedcover, his head on the pillow. The bed was short; Jonas's feet stuck off the end. He rose and moved a chair to support them. Then he lay back down, placed one hand at his chest and the other on his stomach, and tried to feel the flow of his own breath. His shoulders were tight; he tried to unknot them by envisioning the muscles softening. He could feel the grumble of passing subways and decided to think of it as a comforting sound, a lullaby the city was singing, and he breathed in and out and in and out until his body grew gently heavy. He napped.

He awakened effortlessly, as though he'd slept for only five minutes—and maybe that was all it had been. He hadn't checked his watch before he'd drifted. It had been a pure sleep, untroubled by dreams. He woke with total clarity about where he was and why. He felt like a man close to finishing a dense and illuminating novel, one that would leave him changed forever, and as if he needed to think carefully about what to do next because whatever he smelled and tasted and thought and felt would be, in his mind, imprinted on the story's final pages and would be recalled to him every time he thought of the novel itself. He stretched his legs and arms, half-rolled off the bed, sat on the floor, reached into the box of crackers, and pulled one out but hesitated before biting into it. He wondered what he should do with the remaining hours, though he still hadn't checked his watch, so he still didn't know precisely how many hours remained. He decided he'd rather make his plan without thinking of time constraints and then trim or expand the agenda as needed. Yet, by the same token, he couldn't stop thinking about time. He was guessing he still had plenty, not being specific about what "plenty" meant, and had just begun to eat when the tap came on the door.

It must be Masoud; it could only be Masoud. Nevertheless, Jonas moved cautiously toward the door, trying to make his footsteps silent, to prevent his toe joints from cracking as he walked. He leaned forward. The door didn't have a peephole. He hadn't noticed that before. Didn't all doors have peepholes?

"Yes?" he said softly.

"As-salaam alaykum."

"Masoud," Jonas said, unlocking and opening the door.

The two men embraced. Masoud kissed him three times on his cheeks. Masoud smelled fresh and citrusy, like he'd used lime-scented soap. He carried a briefcase and held in his arms a clipboard, a small Qur'an, and a pile of clean clothes, including underwear and socks. Behind Masoud, Jonas saw two men he didn't know who looked to be in their twenties. They were both thin and could have been brothers. One had a scar on his right cheek and pulled a suitcase on wheels. The other carried a video camera and a high-powered portable light.

The martyr's video. It sent a shock through Jonas. It shouldn't have. Though Masoud had never mentioned Jonas making one, he knew about martyr's videos, of course. Somehow he'd thought he wasn't the right sort of *shaheed* for a video. Then again, perhaps he was exactly right. Not looking the part could increase the video's currency as a propaganda tool. But would he be allowed to say whatever he wanted? He hadn't prepared anything.

How, he suddenly wondered, had it come to this, gotten this far?

Masoud followed Jonas's gaze and spoke to the cameraman softly in Arabic. "I asked him to sit outside for a few minutes while we catch up," Masoud said. He took the chair at the foot of Jonas's bed, lifting it with one hand and putting it right outside the door to the apartment, and then he said something else to the cameraman.

The man with the scar, whom Masoud also did not introduce, unzipped the suitcase. From between layers of bubble wrap, he removed the explosive vest tailored especially for Jonas. Jonas remembered going into the back of a dry cleaner's not six blocks from here a month ago. He'd removed his shirt and had his measurements taken by a man in a *thobe* with a closed, silent face, a man who'd barely looked at him. The tailor wrote everything down, the measurements of Jonas's waist, his chest, his armhole. Later, in the shop's front room as Jonas and Masoud prepared to leave, the man handed the paper to a woman Jonas presumed was his wife. She had tiny hands, and although she didn't meet Jonas's eyes, she smiled at the floor in a crooked, distant way. Jonas still remembered that odd smile. He realized then that she was actually the seamstress and that her husband had taken Jonas's measurements because it would have been *haram* for the woman to do so. Now Jonas saw that she'd made what looked like a white cotton wedding vest with three-inch padding all around the middle. The padding, Jonas knew, carried explosives packed with ball bearings. The man put the vest carefully on a hanger in a closet next to the door, said something in Arabic to Masoud, and left, closing the door behind him.

Masoud hugged Jonas again, held him at arm's length, and looked into his face. *"Kayf haalak, habibi?"* he asked.

"Fine," Jonas said. "I'm fine, I'm . . . I'm good. Praise be to Allah."

Masoud gestured to the cot, and both men sat as though it were a couch. "I am honored to be in your presence," Masoud said. "I am also envious that you have been called upon in this way. You are about to make an enormous difference, my brother. What you are doing will give you a position of honor in the kingdom of Allah, glory be upon Him, but it will also save your country. How many people dream of doing something to change the world? You are a hero. And you will be honored not only here but in Yemen, and the Sudan, and Saudi Arabia. Also in the mosques of Kandahar and in Khyber Pass, which you have visited yourself."

Jonas listened silently to the start of what seemed to be a practiced speech. He felt interested but disconnected, as though Masoud were giving the canned spiel to someone else.

"Are you strong within, brother?" Masoud asked.

Jonas nodded once.

"Does anything worry you now?"

Jonas wondered how honest to be. "Missing people." He hesitated. "I worry about disappointing them, but not too much. I think they'll get it after a while. I do worry about the missing part, though."

"You know," Masoud said after a moment, "that you'll be able to watch them from where you are. And time there is different; it will only be the blink of an eyelash before they join you. Also, you know, there are many others there. The richest of pleasures with the most enlightened of beings awaits you."

Jonas was unconvinced by any of this afterlife theology, but that was not what motivated him in the first place, and he had no desire to argue it now, if he ever had. He shrugged and straightened out his legs, stretching them.

"Fighting is ordained for you, though you dislike it, and it may be that you dislike a thing which is good for you and that you like a thing which is bad for you. But Allah knows, glory be upon Him, and you know not," Masoud said, quoting, Jonas guessed, from the Qur'an. "I want to give you two things to carry," he went on. He reached under some papers on his clipboard and removed a small ziplock bag like those that hold children's sandwiches. "This is rare and precious dust from the Dome of the Rock, where Mohammed, blessed be

His name, ascended to Heaven," he said. "Also a paper with a line from the Qur'an to speed your entry."

Jonas took the bag. "Thank you," he said.

"The thanks are to you." Masoud rose and walked toward the coat closet. "You remember," Masoud pointed to the vest, "that you must put it on very carefully. And this." Masoud pulled the detonator from his pocket and held it out as though for inspection. "You are ready, brother."

Jonas nodded. He felt suddenly extremely fatigued. If he changed his mind now, they would probably kill him. It sounded melodramatic, but he believed it. It would be a pointless death then. They might kill his parents, too.

"The money," Masoud said. "Have you decided . . .?"

Jonas knew Masoud was asking if he preferred the ten thousand dollars to go to his mother or his father. Masoud had asked this question before, and Jonas knew he was supposed to pick. He'd been unable to choose, or even think much about it. His parents did not need the dollars that would be paid in compensation. His father had grown wealthy enough, and his mother, while far from rich, never complained of material want. "Vic," he said. "Can you get it to her? I know she's not family, but . . ."

"Victoria? This is what you want? Not your parents?"

"It will give Vic freedom," Jonas said, "to keep dancing. Which is her passion." And it would make her remember him, too. Always.

Masoud studied Jonas a moment, then nodded. "Can you give me her phone number? And her address?"

Jonas recited the information, and Masoud jotted it on the top paper attached to his clipboard. "She will have it, and she will know it is from you. Now, we don't want to take up too much of your time," Masoud said. "I know this is a night of intense preparation for you. Are you ready for the cameraman?"

"I haven't prepared . . . I didn't know . . ."

"*Mafi mushkila*. No problem." Masoud patted his clipboard. "I've written something."

Jonas shook his head. "I don't want—I'd rather just say what I want to in my own words."

"But . . ." Masoud hesitated. "Usually—" He broke off and studied Jonas for a second. "As you wish," he said. He rose, opened the door, and gestured to the cameraman.

They told Jonas to sit on the floor against a white wall. Behind him, they hung a cloth embroidered in gold thread with Arabic calligraphy, a line from the Qur'an.

"What's it say?" Jonas asked.

"'Allah, let us be at their throats, and we ask you to give us refuge from their evil,'" Masoud recited.

The cameraman set up the light, which stood on spindly metal legs, and adjusted it several times. He spoke to Masoud in Arabic, and the two men laughed. Jonas looked at Masoud questioningly. "He doesn't want your face in the shadows at all," Masoud explained. "It's a challenge in this room." Jonas wasn't sure he believed Masoud—perhaps the cameraman had told some joke at his expense—but then he decided this paranoia was unworthy of him, especially now. "I'm going to get a cup of tea first," he said, knowing they would have to wait but willing to allow that because his throat felt dry and he wasn't sure he could talk to a camera without sipping tea. He went to the kitchen and boiled water in a pot. Two chipped mugs stood in a cabinet. He put a bag of green tea in one and poured the water. He sweetened it with a spoonful of raw honey. Then he offered tea to Masoud and the cameraman, but the offer was made without conviction and, because of that or their own sense of urgency, they declined.

"We want to intrude only briefly," Masoud said. "Leave you to your own preparations."

"What will you do with the video?" Jonas asked as he sat cross-legged on the floor and put his cup beside him.

"We'll show it all over the world," Masoud said. "As inspiration and instruction."

Jonas heard the sound of the camera running. "I

am ready," said the cameraman in heavily accented English.

"Wait," said Masoud. He walked to the right of Jonas and waved his arm through the air for a second, some kind of a ritual Jonas didn't understand. He shook his head and then returned to stand next to the cameraman. "Go ahead," he said to Jonas.

Jonas took a sip of the tea. He put down the cup and straightened his back. "Tomorrow I will be a—a martyr," he began. "I will be a martyr, yes, and I want to say . . . well, first, I'm doing this of my own will. It's my free decision." He remembered Masoud had told him once during training that this declaration was important to include in a martyr's video, so he decided to start there. He cleared his throat. "I want to say . . . I love my family. I love my country, too. And Vic. Vic? I love you. So you might wonder . . ." He took a deep breath. *You know why,* he told himself. *Just let it flow.* "Something has gone wrong, seriously wrong, and many of us know it, but many also are sleeping. We have to stand for more than greed and individualism. Many have tried to raise these issues through demonstrations and letter-writing campaigns. But when you look at history, you see that times of critical change are always accompanied by bloodshed." He wondered for a moment if that were completely true, *always accompanied,* or if he should make room for the odd exception, so he added, "Nearly always," and then went on, "It is a failure of the human system that we do not make a shift except when force-fully compelled to do so, and nothing is more per-suasive than violence."

His throat felt extraordinarily dry. He took another sip of tea. "Sorry," he said to Masoud, who nodded encouragingly. The cameraman kept his eye to the lens, so Jonas felt he was being filmed by a camera with legs, with no human involvement at all. "For me, this is an ethical decision," Jonas said, speaking again to the camera. "I love my life in many ways. I love the smell of pine in the woods, and I love . . ." he stumbled momentarily, "damn, I would never take a life without sacrificing my own—that's immoral—and so I'm giving up my own future. That's how strongly I believe in what I'm doing." He ran the fingers of his right hand through the hair on his head, the only hair he still had on his body. "There are no innocents any-more," he said. "We are all complicit. If you are a survivor whose heart aches after this, please take that ache and transform it into change. Question our government. Question our state-sanctioned terrorism. Question the social values that have blinded us to what is real." Jonas real-ized his voice had gotten louder. He paused and made an effort to speak calmly, sanely. "If you are a survivor whose heart aches, reach out and connect with another survivor on the other side of the world and see if together you can find a way to change all that alienates us from each other, and from the earth, and from our God, by whatever name we call Him." He took a deep breath. Masoud leaned forward.

"In the name of the Merciful . . ." he prompted in a stage-whisper.

"So I guess I'm done," Jonas said. "I act in the name of the Merciful, the all-Knowing, all-Seeing. Praise and glory be to Him, to Him belong the credit and the praise."

"Good," Masoud said, and then he actually said, "Cut," which almost made Jonas laugh, though he stopped himself in time.

The camera clicked off. The cameraman emerged from behind the lens and went to close the portable light.

Masoud reached forward to take Jonas's hand, pull him to his feet, and embrace him. "You," he said, "are a powerful man. So much wisdom."

Jonas was starting to forget already whatever it was he had said on camera. He knew he was exhausted. He shook his head to try to clear it. "Oh, well," he said. "Is this the first time you've recorded one of these things in English? And will it be shown, all of it, just as I've said it?" Jonas heard the tinge of doubt in his own voice.

Masoud put a hand on Jonas's shoulder. "Your words are very important, especially following on your deeds." He opened the door and brought the chair back into the apartment. "Now," he said, "I will shave your head."

Jonas sat in the chair in the middle of the room. The cameraman sat on the bed. From his briefcase, Masoud removed scissors, shaving cream, and a professional-looking razor. Masoud stood in front of Jonas for a moment, looking directly into his eyes, and then he hovered over him, and all Jonas heard was the metal sound of the scissors doing their work. He glanced down and saw his long, curly locks falling to the floor and his stomach suddenly felt queasy so he tightened his lips against his teeth and closed his eyes.

It took not more than five or six minutes, and then Masoud put down the scissors. It wasn't Jonas's imagination; his head felt lighter, his neck longer. He opened his eyes and saw that the cameraman had brought a pot full of water and placed it on the floor. Masoud sprayed shaving cream on Jonas's head and began shaving in long, smooth lines, cleaning the razor in the pot of water after every three strokes. He worked silently, with concentration, and his hands felt sure, even nurturing, as they moved across Jonas's scalp. When he finished, Masoud used a towel, also brought by the cameraman, to clean the remaining cream from behind Jonas's ears. Masoud ran his finger over the side of Jonas's head and then sprayed more cream and shaved one more time. Then he put the towel on Jonas's head and massaged his scalp to dry it.

Jonas reached up to feel his head. The skin was rubbery to the touch, like the bottom of a shoe. His scalp tingled. He wanted to go look in a mirror, but that might make him seem too concerned for this world. He would wait. The cameraman was already pulling on his coat, and he said something to Masoud, seeming impatient.

"My brother, I leave you," Masoud said.

"We're done?" Time. Jonas had a sense of time, then, like a snowflake drifting steadily toward the ground. It was so cold today, this last full day of his last winter. It was too cold for snow, even.

"Remember, you are taking the shortest path to heaven," Masoud said. "Do not forget me when you have risen."

For just a moment, Jonas imagined himself a snowflake so light that a breeze could carry it, lifting it higher into the air so that it would rise, reversing the natural order of time, before descending again.

In the moments it took for that thought to occur, Masoud and the cameraman were at the door. They'd almost closed it behind them when Jonas called Masoud's name. Masoud poked his face back into the room.

"Thank you," Jonas said. "You showed me what I could do with all my . . . my disappointment. You showed me this path. I—I'll miss you."

Masoud stared at him a moment and then smiled. "May Allah, glory be upon Him, be with you," he said. "May He give you success so that you achieve Paradise." He closed the door behind him.

Jonas went to the bathroom mirror. Without his hair, he felt exposed. His scalp was whiter than he would have imagined. His eyes seemed larger, his eyebrows an aberration. He looked away from his bald head. His tiredness had by now sunk into his muscles. He hadn't wanted to be alone again—he'd almost feared it, he realized now—but maybe Masoud was right to leave him. Two weeks ago he had felt ready, almost impatient; now he recognized he still needed mental and emotional preparation.

If not for this—this bald head, this vest waiting in the closet—he might have had five decades of vital life ahead, even more. But, given life's arbitrariness, he might have had only five months before dying in some silly, forgettable, meaningless way. Hit by a car as he biked to Central Park, for instance. Become a crime victim and end up on a police report: M/W/21, killed by GSW to torso. So the question became how to best meet the muscular, indestructible strength of death. On *his* terms, he thought. His own terms.

Still, he longed to talk to Vic. Even though she'd moved on, he longed to hear her voice and let her hear his one more time. Everything felt so near now—events from the past and those in the future—that this desire settled in his throat, strong enough to cut off his breath. He locked the door and took his cell phone from under the pillow, and this time he didn't hesitate. He pressed the speed dial that would connect him to Vic and put the phone to his ear. He heard nothing.

He moved to the window. He had strong reception and plenty of battery power. He punched the number again and heard nothing. He tried the speed dial for his mother, and then for his father, and then, staving off desperation, he tried to call a couple of friends he hadn't seen in months, and then he had to admit it: they had disengaged his phone. Anticipating this temptation, they'd somehow disabled his service. They trusted him, but only to a point. And after all, they'd been right.

He took a deep breath.

And it was fine. It was.

He walked toward the corner where he'd been videotaped. Without premeditation, he drew back his bare foot and kicked the chipped mug. He kicked it so hard it banged against the wall. The force of the impact painfully jammed his toes, and he yelled. If Masoud could hear and the yell drew him back to this studio apartment, Jonas would say it had been an accident. But what had been the accident—the toppling of the mug, or all of it? The entire path that had found him chatting with

Masoud about religion, then sleeping in a madrassa, then target-practicing in a rocky field in Pakistan, and now on a mission? He would leave that unspecified, if Masoud were to ask, and then he would see what happened, how Masoud responded.

Or perhaps he would say, "If there is a way, let this cup—this chipped mug—pass from me."

But of course Masoud did not return. Masoud was already far away.

Could the kicking of the mug be a prayer, too?

Jonas fetched the first-aid cream from the bathroom, picked up his camera, and pulled the chair over by the window. He sat down and patted the thick cream gingerly on the top of his injured right foot. He took a snapshot of his foot, then cupped his shaven toes with one hand and curled them around his fingers, resting his shaven chin on his shaven knee. With his left hand, he rubbed a circle on the top of his head, as if comforting himself.

Jonas had intended to carry the first-aid cream with him in the morning. He knew, although he did not want to consider it closely, that afterward individual parts were unlikely to be very large and that even identification might be difficult. He knew that. Nevertheless, standing in the pharmacy earlier today, he'd imagined that the first-aid cream would survive intact and serve as a kind of message demonstrating his innocence and good intentions.

Look, he carried first-aid cream.

Truthfully Jonas couldn't even sort out his thinking about it now. He would probably leave the cream behind, he thought. He was already a different person from the one in the pharmacy.

He looked out the window. A full moon. And he imagined Vic, surely in her apartment on this cold Sunday evening, not that far away, maybe looking out at the moon, too. He could go to her, he just could, and he could explain very briefly. Even if she no longer desired him, they were friends. She would help. Maybe they could manage to get to his parents, and they could all leave. Go to JKF or LaGuardia, catch a flight somewhere.

He felt the tears pressing under his eyelids. He couldn't do that. He wouldn't get away with it, not now; it had gone too far. And even if he did reach Vic and back away from this plan, he would hate himself in a year, hate that he'd had a chance to do something worthwhile, something he believed in, something to match what Deirdre had done, and had been too cowardly to go through with it.

He would write Vic, he decided. It would not be as satisfying as hearing her voice, but it would eliminate the danger of emotion clouding reason, or revealing something he shouldn't, or caving in altogether. He would write her as part of his final preparation, and he would photograph his hand holding a pen and moving across a page, and he would write them all—not only Vic but his parents, Deirdre, two or three of his teachers, maybe even the funny ex-monk Harold—and he would mail the letters in the morning on his way to the subway. Afterward the words would arrive along with the smudges he left on the pages and the scent of his tiny last apartment on the Avenue of the Finest, all of it carried on a breeze of its own.

And, yes, that would surely be a prayer.

NEW YORK: 8:38 P.M.
MECCA: 4:38 A.M.

Vic picked up her cell phone and stared at the screen for what had to be the twentieth time, checking to see if somehow she'd missed its ring. Odd that Jonas hadn't called back yet. Of course, that probably wouldn't have made her nervous if Jonas's mother hadn't come visiting with her own set of fears. What was there to worry about? Jonas wasn't in trouble. More likely he'd simply met someone else. Vic had opened him up, primed him for love, and—even worse—sat around fantasizing about him, and then he'd met some girl on campus who could taste his sweet sensitivity and shy smile and long, lovely body, and they were together now, lying on her narrow bed in a tiny room, a candle flickering on the dresser, her textbooks scattered on a wooden desk carved with someone else's initials, street noises floating through the window they'd cracked open to let some cool air bathe their sweaty skin. And Jonas, naked, was saying to her, this other woman, a close version of the things he'd said to Vic, and that Vic had foolishly hoped were intended for her alone.

Jonas was not really like that, she told herself, and yet she knew men, by their nature, were different from women. This knowledge was part of what made her so cautious. Men had this whole thing about the chase, and then the opportunity, and no matter how much they loved one woman, no matter how great she was, given a chance with another, they'd feel it sinful to say no, if they even for a second considered refusing. They deemed it their right—their duty, maybe—and the physical always took precedence over the emotional. Men thought as long as they were having sex, they couldn't be counted among the lonely, the aging, or the pathetic. Women knew otherwise.

Vic did not consider her viewpoint extreme. She'd drawn her conclusions by watching her mother and her father. For months on end, the two of them would leave for work in the morning, laughing over something, and he'd be home on time for dinner, and they'd wash the dishes together and go out to movies. Then her father would start mentioning a particular female author or an editor, and then he'd stop mentioning her altogether—the giveaway—and work would begin to preoccupy him more than usual, and then he would come home late with a face made rosy by joy and guilt, and it was all so clear. Vic would have known what was happening even if she hadn't caught him on the phone, or in his office the afternoon when she'd walked in unannounced, and even if he hadn't finally moved out. He was a good man, her father. She admired him in many ways. She was even like him, partly. This was simply the way it went and the way it always would go between men and women. Time without end.

Mara was still too young to have figured all this out, and certainly too young to have made peace with it. Thinking of this made Vic deeply indignant, for her mother, for herself, but mostly for Mara. Vic still remembered seeing her sister for the first time in the hospital—a miracle, she'd thought, as she'd inhaled the scent of newness that still clung to the infant, overpowering the antiseptic hospital smell. Their mother had gone back to work quickly, which had increased Vic's sense of responsibility for this infant with prematurely wise eyes. She spent long hours rocking the baby. She grew as anxious as she imagined any mother would when Mara, at eight months, became sick with a wheezing cough. Every night until Mara got better, she crept into the baby's room and slept on the floor, and nothing her parents said could dissuade her. When she was sixteen and desperate for independence, Mara was the one who kept her tied to family.

One night about a week after their parakeet died, Mara came to Vic. "What does that mean, to die?"

Where the hell, thought Vic, *are Mom and Dad when you need them?*

"Will it happen to me?" Mara asked.

Vic sighed. "It's a long way off."

"Will I have to leave all of you behind?"

"Hey, we'll probably go first. Age-wise, it's Dad, then Mom, then me. You're last, angel."

"You'll die?" Mara's eyes were dry but very wide.

"Oh, damn. Crawl into bed," Vic said. "We'll talk about it later."

Only they never did. Vic picked up the phone and called what she still considered, on some level, to be her home number. Mara answered on the second ring.

"Angel, where are you?"

"In bed."

"And where's Mom?"

"In her room. You want me to get her?"

"No, I'm calling for you. I'm calling to make sure you're almost asleep," Vic said. "You've got school tomorrow."

"I know."

Her voice sounded odd. Strained. "You okay?" Vic asked.

"I'm all right." But she didn't sound all right.

"Are you sad, sweetheart?" Vic asked.

"I'm okay," Mara said. "I'm just—I don't know, Vic. I turned out the lights, and I felt so scared I turned them back on again."

"What scared you?" Vic said.

"It felt like air was blowing past my face. A hard, hot wind. I felt it even when I went under the covers."

"And now?"

189

"Now it's gone."

"Maybe a heating vent is aimed at your bed?"

"No," Mara said.

"Okay, then maybe you should sleep with a light on. How about the one over your desk?"

"Sure." Mara's voice sounded very quiet and far away.

"I wish I were there right now."

"I wish so, too," said Mara.

Vic felt deeply guilty then. She hadn't been paying enough attention to Mara. She hadn't done enough to help her adjust to the new home situation. "I'm coming over tomorrow for dinner," she said. "If I possibly can, that is. If Alex doesn't make the rehearsal go on forever. Which I don't think he will. He's usually pretty mellow about our last night. So I'm coming over and we'll make enchiladas, okay?" The line was quiet. "Okay, Mara?" Vic said.

"Okay," Mara said.

"Good-night, baby."

As soon as she was off, Vic called her father's number. "Dad," she said.

"Vic. I'm so glad to hear from you." The enthusiasm in his voice felt like hype. Either someone was in the room with him—which she didn't want to know about—or he was ridiculously hopeful that a phone call from Vic meant his life without Mom was falling into place and that the change was being accepted by his family.

"I'm worried about Mara," she said.

Her father didn't respond immediately. "Go ahead," he said after a moment.

"She's having bad dreams. She isn't eating well. Mom is too upset to feed her. She's under a lot of stress."

Her father sighed. "I'm sorry, Vic."

"Yeah, we're both sorry," Vic said. "But right now she needs a little more than that. Remember, she's only eleven. You forget that because Mara is so—well, so *Mara*. I know she tests off the charts and even in first grade, she was like this baby adult, but this—this thing—it's beyond her." *And you're responsible for it,* Vic wanted to say, but she stopped herself, adding instead, "I think you should go there—tomorrow morning. Have breakfast with her. Or something. Listen to her. Find out what's going on for yourself."

Again the line fell silent for a beat. "You're right," her father said. "I'll go. I'll go before school. I'll let your mom know tonight."

Vic felt gratified by the response, but she was unwilling to sound too pleased. "It can't just be a one-shot deal, either, Dad. You can dump Mom, but you can't dump Mara." Normally she wouldn't talk like that to her dad, but she knew he wouldn't say anything.

"I've only been staying away out of respect to your mother, who needs her space right now."

"I'm unconvinced that it's Mom who needs the

space but—" Her father started to respond, so she just spoke over him, "but it's not my business, and I don't even really care. I just don't want Mara feeling bad. Beyond that, I leave it to you and Mom. Beyond that, you can call me when the shooting's over."

"All right, Vic," her father said. "Okay. I respect that."

Vic hung up and lay back on the couch, flexing her feet. The emptiness of her apartment seemed large and forceful, so when she heard someone come into the building, she jumped to her feet and flung open her front door, thinking it might be Jonas.

It was her upstairs neighbor. Jackie, who worked for the MTA, was undereducated but smart and saw the funny side of everything. She invariably had comic subway stories to tell. She had a daughter in middle school and another in high school, and every Thanksgiving, the oldest girl brought Vic a homemade loaf of the most moist, tasty pumpkin bread she'd ever had.

"Hi, Vic, how you doing?" Jackie called.

Vic leaned against the doorframe. "Long day?"

"The longest. And I got to be back in at seven o'clock in the morning."

"Anything interesting happen today?" Vic asked, because she wasn't ready to go back into her room and lose all direct human contact again.

"Some man asked me how to get to the Sears

Tower. Can you imagine? I said, 'Take a plane to Chicago.' "

"You're making this up."

"And two teenaged boys were stopped trying to jump over the turnstile directly in front of three cops. Where were their heads?"

Vic laughed.

"The station was crawlin' with them today. Cops, I mean. When's your show open, hon?"

"Tuesday," Vic said. "I'll snag you three tickets for next weekend if you want them."

"We'd love 'em. Watching you dance makes me feel hope for the world."

Vic's phone began ringing and she turned to it quickly. "See you, Jackie." This had to finally be Jonas, but she wasn't going to jinx it by looking at caller ID.

"Hello?" she said.

"Victoria."

"Yes?"

"This is Masoud. Masoud al-Zufak."

"Oh, yes. Jonas's . . ."

"I just wanted to let you know I'll be mailing you something. Please keep your eye out for it."

Vic had begun pacing as Masoud spoke. "An invitation or something?" she asked.

"It should arrive in three days."

"Do you need my address?'

"Jonas gave it to me."

"Jonas?" Her voice rose. "Is Jonas—"

"May the night watch over you, Victoria."

"Wait, wait, wait," she said, but Masoud hung up as she was speaking.

She went to the kitchen to pour herself a glass of water. She unexpectedly felt like crying. "What the hell is this?" she said aloud as she filled a mug from the sink. Then she inhaled deeply. *Get a grip. Jonas doesn't return a couple calls and you start imagining all sorts of nonsense. After all, you didn't call him for days, either.*

She sipped her water, looking out the window. The moon, so often hidden by neighboring buildings, was clearly visible, a half-moon that made her think of what she had. She was a professional dancer, and that had always been her dream, ever since elementary school, and although she was not rich she could pay her rent, and she'd tasted this amazing flavor with Jonas, this flavor of profound love, even if it had turned out to be brief, and she had a whole life ahead of her with all kinds of unexpected pleasures, and she was still young and healthy and essentially hopeful, living in this amazing city filled with remarkable people, at the center of the earth.

Carol refrained from flipping on the lights in the kitchen, both out of courtesy to Jake, who she could hear softly snoring in the living room, and because she liked working in the semi-dark, by the light of the refrigerator as she removed the milk and then by the light of the stove as she warmed the milk and stirred in a spoonful of honey. After her mug was ready, she slipped into the living room, steering wide of the couch, where she could see his form under the blanket, and moved to a small armchair she kept near the window. Below, she could see the lights of the passing cars and hear their murmur. It was soothing, a citified way of watching the ocean, feeling its timelessness.

"Couldn't sleep?"

Jake's voice startled her. It was tender with grogginess. She hadn't heard that voice in a long time. "Sorry," she said. "I woke you."

He sat up, wrapping the blanket around him. "I wasn't really sleeping," he said.

She laughed softly. "You were snoring."

"That's what I do when I'm not sleeping," he said. He scooted over to one end of the couch and patted the spot next to him. "Sit here. I won't bite."

She looked down toward the street for another

moment, then decided that to refuse would be churlish. "Want some warm milk?" she asked.

"I'll have a sip of yours."

She sat on the couch and held her mug out to him. "You know, Jake," she said as he was drinking, "sometimes I wonder if we made a mistake."

"Splitting up?"

"Raising Jonas outside any spiritual tradition."

"We decided those spiritual traditions left a lot to be desired, and we were right."

"And then we let him take that year and just wander around Europe."

"To recharge his batteries. Help him get re-motivated for school."

"And then I . . ."

"He's a grown man, Carol."

"Did I somehow fail to give him enough . . . structure?"

"Don't torture yourself," he said softly.

"He's always been probing, as though there's one right answer and if he just searches long enough, he'll find it. I think the search has been torturous for him. I think he's felt alone, and lost. I think he hasn't been able to turn to us because he feels we don't understand—and in a way, he's right."

"The young are always searching," Jake said. "That's their job. We searched, remember?"

"Did we?"

He handed her the mug. "We weren't happy with the lives our parents led. What children are? We thought them stilted, boring, corrupt. That was before we recognized the fragility of human judgments."

"But there's something more desperate about what Jonas seems to feel," Carol said. "And I don't remember us being so depressed."

"It's all more serious now," Jake said. "We had a certain innocence; we had that gift. This is the end of the empire. Innocence has already been killed off."

Carol sighed and leaned back into the couch. "You remember Jenny?"

"Your old roommate Jenny?" Yes, he remembered. Jenny had had a son, three years older than Jonas. The summer he was thirteen, they were vacationing somewhere in the Midwest, and he dove into a quarry full of water, hit his head, and drowned.

"I saw her a couple years ago," Carol said. "She told me there's no recovery when you lose a kid. There's only a before and an after."

"Carol." Jake reached over and touched the back of her neck.

"And blame. She talked about blaming herself, that she should have discussed quarries with him, warned him somehow. That she was, in the end, a bad mother, because she failed at the really only important job. She couldn't keep her child safe.

And I understand. If something were ever to go wrong with Jonas—"

"Don't. Don't talk about this now."

She turned to him. "He was the first thing, Jake. That little baby: the first thing besides ourselves we were ever responsible for."

"I'm just," he hesitated, "I'm just going to rub your neck. Okay?"

Carol willed her shoulders to soften; nothing could be done tonight. And in the end, everything would be fine, wouldn't it? Kids scare their parents, but it would all be fine. She dropped her head and felt herself breathe. Jake massaged the back of her neck for a few minutes and then began moving his fingers into her scalp.

"Feel good?"

"Hmmm," she murmured.

Jake's hands. Carol remembered many things about those hands. Maybe she remembered everything about them—although he'd be a little too self-satisfied if he knew that. She used to love to massage his hands, seek out pressure points, tug gently on his fingers. She loved, too, watching those hands when he painted. And he'd taken up carpentry at one point—she still had in her bedroom a little table he'd made. He had capable hands—capable in every way.

She remembered how vulnerable she'd felt when he'd left, and how that vulnerability had remained with her for months—for years, actually. It had taken her a few months just to recover from the surprise that they actually weren't going to make it, that she'd chosen someone with whom she couldn't last, and then she'd lost faith in her own judgment. She'd hidden it, though, because she had Jonas. Without Jonas, she might have fallen apart and climbed into bed for weeks, maybe months. Jonas had saved her from that.

"I feel better, thank you," she said, and straightened her head.

He dutifully pulled his hands into his lap. "Thank *you*," he said.

"For what?"

"Letting me stay tonight."

She sipped her milk, now cool. "It's nice having you here, Jake. For tonight."

"You're magnificent, Carol. You really are."

She made a scoffing sound. "I was more magnificent at thirty-two," she said, "when you left me."

"You know . . ." He hesitated. "You know what that was about, don't you?"

"Oh, Jake. I shouldn't have brought it up."

"Let me say it," he said. "Let me say it because I want you to hear it. I promise I'll only say it once, and then I'll never say it again."

She rotated her shoulders. "My neck is clenching again," she said with a short laugh.

"I left because . . ." He took a deep breath. "Because I found out I couldn't paint. I wasn't a painter."

Now she laughed harder. "That feels like a reason that required some hours to invent."

"We went into adulthood together, you and I," he said. "And like Jonas, we had our idealism. Our dreams. You realized yours. You became a successful potter, it seemed like in a matter of weeks. You had that show Lily sponsored, and then you were off."

"I always loved your work," she said.

He shook his head. "It wasn't going anywhere. I realized I didn't have an artistic vision. How could I? I didn't know where I wanted it to go. I saw I was better at appreciating art than producing it."

"Jake," she said, "I really don't want to spend much time here, but for the sake of honesty—all blame aside, after all it's been years—what you realized you appreciated was that painter. What was her name?" Only that last line, Carol thought, was dishonest. She *knew* the painter's name, though she wished she could have forgotten. Sarah Lyster.

"She was a consolation prize, nothing more," Jake said. "I knew I was going to fail you, and then lose you."

"You make me sound like a shrew-wife. I never put that kind of pressure on you."

Jake held his head in both his hands and rubbed his scalp. His blond hair was graying, but he still had a full head of it. And in the moonlight that overflowed through the window, he looked so much like a little boy that, for a second, Carol felt her heart break. She looked down into the mug of milk, trying to harden herself. He'd always had the ability to affect her this way, to turn her to liquid. The fact was, she'd known all along that she was the best thing he'd ever find. That they fitted together in ways that went beyond logic, beyond words. And still she had to stand aside and watch him screw it up. And then she had to patch herself back together. And she did it. But even though the glue held, the crack remained visible—to her eye, at least.

"We'd created this dream about what we were meant to be together," he said, "and I could see that, because of me, it wasn't going to play out as we'd envisioned. I'd have ended up disappointing you."

She cleared her throat and drained her voice of emotion. "And your having an affair was supposed to be less disappointing than giving up painting and opening an art gallery?"

"Look, I don't say I handled it well; I don't say I handled it with complete self-knowledge. But a few years of therapy later, at least I understand *why* I squandered what I had. Why meeting your eyes suddenly became so difficult. And—I'm sorry, Carol."

This apology was a first, and something Carol hadn't anticipated. They sat for a few minutes, silent. Carol listened to a siren from below. She heard the elevator pass her floor on the way down. Thinking about the time lost with this big, foolish, brilliant bear of a man beside her, she felt a flood pushing at the back of her eyes. She was glad it was too dark for him to see.

"I don't think you have anything to be ashamed of in the choices you made," she said when she could talk normally. Then she clarified: "The *professional* choices, I mean."

He laughed. "The personal ones are another matter, then?"

She sighed. "If it weren't that, you know, it might have ended up being something else that came between us. How many people stay together decade after decade in this country?"

"Mmm."

"We're lucky we shared what we did; I still feel that. And we had Jonas."

"Jonas." Jake nodded, reaching out to squeeze Carol's knee.

"And now." She rose. "I should try to get to sleep. So should you."

He stood up with her and held out his arms, and she let herself sink into them, and she let him embrace her. She felt how the shape of him had changed since he'd last hugged her like this, how he'd thickened and softened, and she put her head against his chest and felt his breath, and she joined him, one, two, three, four, five breaths. She gave herself that. And then she disengaged herself and touched his cheek and said good-night and went to bed, not to sleep but to lie and think and talk aloud and wait until the morning brought what it would.

Sonny tugged down his ski cap until it met his
eyebrows and then, trying to steal heat from
within his own body, breathed heavily in the
direction of the scarf circled twice around his
neck. The moist air from his mouth landed mainly
on his beard, where it did little more than add to
the slender icicles already dangling from his chin-
hairs. Thank God, at least, for that last serving of
hot stew Ruby had dished out before he'd left, and
the knitted scarf she'd handed him on his way out
the door. "Blessed scarf," he'd called it, kissing it
and bowing before her, and she'd laughed.
Swathed in maroon wool, his neck felt itchy but
cozy enough. The rest of him, though, was plenty
grateful when he spotted the green symbol of the
metro station ahead. Home. Hurrying past white
steam rising thickly from the darkness of a man-
hole, he scrambled down the stairs, a squirrel
diving for its burrow.

A cold of a clammier sort circulated underground, but it felt more bearable than above,
where the greedy wind tried to strip naked anybody foolish or desperate enough to be out. A cop
stood on the other side of the turnstile, holding a
nightstick in his right hand and tapping it against
his left palm, beating a nameless tune like a musi-

cian with a mission. It was O'Neil, a middle-aged sergeant with a worn face plenty firm, but generous, too. Sonny had grown to like O'Neil over the years and thought the feeling was mutual. Dutifully, and a little showy-like, Sonny pulled a MetroCard out of his back pocket and ran it through the machine, trying to look virtuous. O'Neil shook his head with a slight smile, silently signaling that Sonny wasn't putting one over on him, that he knew Sonny had used a dime to crease his card and get in for free, just like they all did. No way O'Neil could bust him, though, since there was no proving it.

"Morning, officer," Sonny said. "Awful cold and early for you to be out."

"Sonny." O'Neil nodded a greeting. "Still kicking, I see."

"Yessiree. Ain't your usual hours, are they, O'Neil?"

"Ain't hours I want, either. They're a bit jumpy at headquarters this week. They got us doing all kinds of crazy things."

"These times," Sonny said, shaking his head sympathetically. "How's the family?"

O'Neil smiled. "Oldest boy got a scholarship to SUNY-Purchase," he said. "Happy as he can be. Studying philosophy or some damn thing, but the wife is happy, too, because he's so close."

"Kids heading out into the world. Means you done well," Sonny said.

O'Neil shrugged. "Hey, Sonny," he said, "you hear they're doling out blankets next Saturday morning at the Church of the Redemption, right above the Atlantic Street station?"

"Can't say I did."

"Might get yourself on over there. Farmer's Almanac says it's going to be a cold one."

"Just might do that, thanks." Sonny nodded and headed downstairs toward the uptown F-train. Another officer stood on the platform. He wasn't anyone Sonny knew, so he shuffled on by and sat on the bench.

Weekends, the platform would be crowded at this hour, full of clubbers headed home. Sonny didn't mind the late-night company, though it did bother him that his visitors, after hours spent yelling over music, were often still speaking in too-loud voices. It was the time and place, after all, to be respectful—if not of other passengers, at least of sleeping children and the dead.

Weeknights were a different, quieter story. Tonight, except for the officer and Sonny, only one other person stood on the platform: a young Hispanic woman wearing fingerless gloves, black pants, and a thick jacket embroidered with the initials TSA. Transport Security Administration. Sonny guessed she was headed home after a shift at one of the airports, checking bags, looking for terrorists. She probably wasn't much over twenty years old. Pinned to her jacket was an inch-high plastic teddy bear, the kind of trinket you might expect to see worn by a little girl. Her eyes were sleepy slits, and her lips seemed welded together. She'd clogged her ears with tiny headphones, listening to some beat pumped directly into her brain to cut out the rest of the world. Sonny didn't like those machines. Especially when he was working, because the digital music players made it too easy for people to overlook both his need and the opportunity he offered them.

But his objection to these devices was larger and less self-serving than that. He appreciated that this was a cauldron of a city and that sometimes, especially trapped in the subway—the bowels, some called it—folks were forced to stare straight at something that might be jarring or even alarming, something they thought they should escape from. But in Sonny's view, it served better to consider the subway as a pot of the most delicious soup imaginable, warming the soul on the cold night and chock-full of ingredients both exotic and common. Some people were the garlic or pepper—unpleasant when eaten by itself. But they were just as necessary to the soup as the chicken and carrots. And having to eat a spoonful of that soup broadened folks, taught 'em tolerance, gave 'em appreciation for folks living closer to the edge, or higher on the hog, or whatever was the opposite of their understanding of life. To Sonny's mind, those earphones flat weren't good for the human race.

Sonny sat on a bench and considered his evening plans. He wasn't too tired because he'd taken a nap at Ruby's. Still, given the right spot, it would suit him to catch a couple hours. A place that smelled harmless enough and offered protection from drafts but wasn't so far out of the way that he might be jumped. Underground held a fair share of good sleeping spots. Tonight he felt in the mood for the 4th Street station. One particular stretch of concrete, in fact, that he knew would give him privacy while supporting his weary body for a bit.

The train pulled in, and Sonny, the police officer, and the TSA employee all got on, each choosing a different car. Sonny's car held only one other person: a black transvestite with a bouffant wig. As the train began to move, he—looking very much like a she—rose and sauntered past Sonny, hips swaying almost as if he were a model on a catwalk. He wore a long coat, which he kept open in the front to reveal a silky red dress that couldn't be keeping him warm. He was well padded; his curves looked authentic. He had nice eyes, too, Sonny saw. Only the black high-laced tennis shoes seemed misplaced. He stopped about three feet away from Sonny, took hold of a high handrail, and flexed his shoulders. Two stops later, he turned around and headed Sonny's way again, studying him carefully. A couple got on and moved to the far end of the car. The transvestite slid into a seat opposite Sonny, staring openly now. Sonny sat easy, a noncommittal expression on his face, knowing it was best to wait it out, let the fellow finish whatever strutting was needed. The transvestite leaned forward and said in the most feminine voice Sonny could imagine, "You de best thing I've seen in a while."

Sonny chuckled. "Then that ain't no good for you."

"Name's Murilee," the man-woman said. "You looking for some warmth, some help passing this winter night?"

"Don't be thinking so," Sonny said.

"Won't even charge you much for it. Maybe just a cuppa coffee afterward."

There was a time, Sonny thought. Time he might'a said yes to this self-created, self-named person who inclined hopefully toward him. Might'a said yes even though he knew that once they were alone together, a dingy padded bra would fall off to reveal a concave chest, and the legs, shaven but still a man's, would take him back some, and as for the equipment itself, it would be a long way from his dreams. He'd'a said yes despite the shortcomings because people had those days when they felt pretty self-sufficient, and then they had those days when they were needy as a babe. Whether they slept on a bed or a bench, didn't matter. Everybody had days like that. Loneliness pulled at every part of you, and sixty seconds of adoration, even paid for, seemed the only chance you had at keeping the pieces from flying off in all directions.

"Not tonight," he said to Murilee. "Thank ye, though."

"Oooh," Murilee said. "A polite refusal. You're making my blood run hot."

Sonny chuckled, and then, seeing the train pull into 4th Street, he rose. "Good-night, now," he said. "Be safe."

"Rather be sexy than safe," Murilee said, and laughed, low and husky, with cracks that allowed the masculine to peek through. That was the last sweet noise Sonny heard as the train doors closed and the subway sped away.

Sonny passed another couple of cops talking together in low voices as he made his way up one set of stairs. Now he was one level beneath ground instead of two. The cleaners had already come blasting through, pointing their power spray, and the air smelled of trapped disinfectant, which suited Sonny just fine. Fresh as he was now, he sure didn't want to lie down someplace that had seen toilet-use. He headed for the stretch he wanted, slightly beyond the edge of the platform. It was a slender ledge, narrow as a chastity bed, and in all the times he'd slept there, nobody'd ever tried to run his pockets, so he considered it safe enough.

As he approached, though, he saw that somebody had taken over his spot. A huddled lump using a pile of newspapers as mattress and a flowered sheet as comforter. Sonny had never seen another person lying in his spot before. He hovered above the form. After a minute, it shifted slightly. Something poked out its head.

"Benny," Sonny said without a spitful of warmth.

"Sonny." Benny let his head drop back down to the cement. "Glad it's you. Thought it was someone trying to split my wig, but I'm so weak, I'd just have to let 'em go at it."

"What's wrong?" Sonny asked.

Benny pulled the sheet under his chin. "Not feeling too good."

"You junk-sick?" Sonny knew he didn't sound overly sympathetic.

"No, man, no way. Got meself the flu, I think."

"Got to man up, Benny," Sonny said dryly.

"Can't," Benny said, and pulled the sheet over his face.

Sonny grunted. He didn't much like Benny. The Wheelchair Robber, he was nicknamed. Benny gave folks like Sonny a bad name. Benny had two props: a wheelchair and a pile of funny stories about the city. Come nightfall, he would park aboveground near the entrance to one subway or another, telling his stories, calling out until people gathered, and then passing the hat. The lame storyteller. That was fine by Sonny, but it wasn't much of a living for Benny, so he'd developed a less savory habit. From time to time, often enough to get a reputation among his underground colleagues, Benny was approached by some tourist—he always targeted a woman—who was visiting from China or Connecticut and didn't know exactly where she was, or didn't pay attention when she leaned toward Benny, or stood too close when she turned her back to him. That was when he would reach into a purse, or sometimes a pocket, and lift the bread, or a cell phone, or whatever shit he could find. Benny had been doing it for years now, so his switch from beggar to thief back to beggar again was as rapid as an addict's mood swings. His victim rarely noticed right away that she'd been robbed, but as a safety measure, Benny always shoved the stolen goods directly under his butt and wheeled away immediately so that if she turned around for one last look at the poor lame storyteller, he was gone. And on the rare occasion when someone caught him and yelled out, he sprang up and dashed off down the street, fast as a relay racer. Then the passersby could see he didn't need that wheelchair after all, except to build his audience's trust. All this took its toll on public opinion of men like Sonny and the younger ones who played drums or break-danced—all those trying to make an honest living in the subways. It was as if Benny robbed them, too.

Now Benny shifted his body and groaned, then peeked out one red-rimmed eye. "Might be pneumonia." He shivered as if to prove his point. "No health insurance, either, ha. You don't have an extra blanket, do ya?"

Sonny laughed. "Yeah. Right here in my dresser."

"What I need is Mrs. Wu," Benny said. "If I weren't so weak and frail, I'd go myself." He lifted his head and shot Sonny a hopeful look.

"Jesus, Benny." Sonny shook his head and stared down onto the tracks, where a rat was trying to move what looked like a stale hunk of bread.

"You do it for me, won't you, Sonny? You aren't like most of 'em."

Sonny shrugged off the attempt at flattery. "First you be in my place, and now you want to put me on an errand. You been drinking smiley juice, Benny?"

"I'm sure she's in Rockefeller Center right behind the tollbooth, just like always. It only take you twenty, twenty-five minutes round-trip."

"I don't know what watch be telling you that."

"Besides, you's her favorite."

Sonny shook his head again but started back to the platform. At least Benny wasn't crazy or savage-like; Sonny had to appreciate that. Besides, he was family of sorts. "Damn good thing I'm subway-loyal, Benny. I only hope she's there," he said over his shoulder.

The train came pretty quickly, and Rockefeller Center was only four stops away. It was one of the busier stations, always well lit, and that probably explained why Mrs. Wu made it her place. Mrs. Wu looked to be about forty-five, which probably meant she was thirty-four. Homeless life aged folks fast, especially the women. She carried four or five bags always, and whenever somebody in the underground community needed something home-like—needle and thread, hot-water bottle, loofah sponge—they went to find Mrs. Wu. Mrs. Wu wasn't a bottle lover; far as Sonny knew, she was one of the street people who stayed straight, but she wasn't always *there,* either. Sonny'd seen her eyes glaze and her mind get lost someplace else, so she couldn't even hear him talking to her. Story Sonny heard was that she owned her own home once but lost it four or five years ago. He didn't know if that was true. He didn't know if she had children, or even if she really was a married woman, even though folks called her *missus.* It wasn't polite to nosy into how things had gone wrong for a body.

She was there behind the booth, asleep, lying on top of two bags of belongings, holding a third under her arm like some stuffed toy, and leaning against a fourth. Sonny gently shook her arm.

"How you doin', mama?" She was younger than Sonny by some twenty years, but that was what he always called her. Meant as a compliment.

"Wha'? Wha'?" She rubbed her eyes and sat up stiffly. "Oh, Sonny. I thought you were cops again, trying to move Mrs. Wu."

"How you doin'?" Sonny asked again, hoping to judge her state of mind.

"Mrs. Wu well enough," she said.

"Well, Benny's sick," Sonny said. "He sent me to ask if you had an extra blanket."

"For Benny, no." She smoothed the hair off her forehead with one hand. "But for you . . ." She reached into the bag that had been under her feet and then stuck her whole head in and rummaged around. "Take two. That way you have one." She handed him a blanket that was sky-blue and very thin, probably made of cotton, and another that was tan, thicker and wool, with three fist-sized holes in the middle.

"Thank ye," said Sonny.

"Want coffee before you go?" Mrs. Wu asked, and Sonny knew this was her way of asking him to buy her a cup.

"You stay here," he said. "I be right back." He walked around the corner and ordered two small cups with cream and sugar.

She was leaning against the tollbooth when he returned. She didn't meet his eyes but looked pleased to see the coffee, smiling in the direction of his feet. She took the cup and wrapped both hands around it like it was a precious jewel she was raising to the sky, and then she put it to her lips, her elbows splayed wide, and held the liquid in her mouth for a long time before swallowing. He sat down beside her.

"You seen Ricky lately?" she asked, and he thought about how so many of them called each other by boyhood names, as if they were stuck in that time, which many of them were, and how Mrs. Wu's role of mother figure had nothing to do with her age, either. They talked for a few minutes about mutual acquaintances who lived and worked underground before Sonny rose to go.

"Wait, Sonny. Something worrying Mrs. Wu." She motioned for him to lean closer and spoke in a quiet voice. "Lots of police around here lately. You notice this?"

"Yes, mama, I have."

She grimaced. Mrs. Wu liked the police less than all the rest of them combined, though Sonny didn't know the source of that aversion. "Everybody jumpy," she said, her voice still hushed. "You know why, Sonny?"

"Why you asking me?" he said.

"Sometime you know things," she said. "Mrs. Wu see this."

Maybe Mrs. Wu was just talking to him because she wanted company a little longer. But her words were a splash of cold water to his face; they made him remember how he'd felt Sunday morning, and now he felt it all again, the air vibrating with sharp but unnamed tension. He didn't want to mention it, though, and wouldn't know how to explain it, anyway.

"You know what it be, mama," he said, trying to sound comforting. "They show up some days, and they nowhere around others. They operate by some clock that only they looking at. It don't mean much to us, after all."

"You think so?" she asked. "They won't round us up?"

The police carried out periodic roundups, dumping homeless folks at dirty and dangerous shelters as though it were a good deed, but it had been a while since that had happened. "Don't think that's it, mama," he said, almost wishing that it were, almost thinking that might be better than whatever lay ahead.

"Hope you right, Sonny. It too cold for Mrs. Wu, I dying outside in this weather. I look after a lot of people, but they don't look after me. So you hear different, you come warn Mrs. Wu, okay?"

"I promise, mama," he said. "I hear anything, I come for you."

She pinched his cheek lightly. "Take care, now, Sonny."

He estimated it took him twenty-five minutes to get back. Benny was still there, half-asleep. Sonny threw the sky-blue blanket over him, and Benny looked up. "Thank ye, Sonny," he said, polite-like, as if he were Sonny's child.

"Well," Sonny said, "scoot back some. Make room. I need to catch some meself."

Benny, still prone, pushed himself back so that his head lay deeper into the tunnel, and Sonny wrapped himself up in the tan blanket and cozied up close the wall, his feet reaching toward Benny's, Ruby's blessed scarf draped over his eyes, warm enough, full enough, but with Mrs. Wu's worries running laps in his head.

Mara woke with a start and poked her head out from under the covers. She was relieved to find that the air felt calm, windless. The lamp above her desk cast a yellow light. Not the cheerful yellow of fresh lemons. Instead it was pale, nostalgic, the yellow of grainy faded photographs and rainy afternoons. She sat up in bed, reaching for her glasses and then the alarm clock. Though the clock verified her suspicion that the hour was too early, she got up anyway.

Mara studied herself for a minute in a mirror that hung next to her door. She'd gotten in the habit lately of inspecting her image each morning, searching for change. She'd grown curious to know if her face was transforming in response to all the other outside changes. And this morning she wanted to know if the sense of responsibility that made her stomach clench had modified her physically somehow. Miraculously—it seemed to her to be a miracle—she still just looked like Mara.

One very specific issue worried Mara this morning. Since Aaron had offered to help with the subway, she was not concerned about getting lost. She could count on him for that. And she knew her father would not be angry with her for coming and that he would hurry to the street and guide her to his apartment on St. Johns and Kingston. What bothered her was whether or not she could be persuasive enough. It had seemed so reasonable at lunch yesterday to imagine that a few rocks might make the difference, but since then, she'd recognized that a lot depended on what she said and how she said it. She realized she was going to have to have an adult conversation with her father, and she hoped that her words would be clear and strong enough that he would be able to make an adjustment in how he saw her, or at least in how he listened to her, so he didn't dismiss her as his little angel and try to comfort her with a rocking hug or a soothing nonsense rhyme.

It had been left to Mara to rescue her mother. No one else seemed to realize the seriousness of the situation. Mara was reminded of a movie she'd watched once with Aaron, one of the few movies they'd seen together that didn't have anything to do with the New York subway system. The title had long since slipped from her memory, but what she did recall was that a ship went down and two women found themselves in a lifeboat with nothing to eat or drink. They floated alone at sea. At first there were jokes, or attempts at jokes, and then singing, and finally the sharing of secrets that altered the way the two women felt about each other and themselves. But as their situation became increasingly desperate, much of the talking ended. One woman finally succumbed to thirst and, though her companion begged her not to, began frantically gulping seawater cupped in her hands. And that drove her mad. It caused sodium toxicity—Mara looked it up afterward—which resulted in a shrinkage of brain cells, which in turn resulted in confusion. The woman, now crazed, jumped into the ocean thinking she was walking into the kitchen in her own home to get a snack. She drowned. The audience was meant to weep for her. But Mara cried for the woman left behind, sane still but alone, floating on the vast sea. Mara felt as if her mother had become the dehydrated woman guzzling saltwater, and Mara was in danger of being abandoned at sea.

It occurred to her that she needed to pray. Yet she had no idea how to do it. No one in her family ever talked about prayer. It seemed an old-fashioned ritual, something vaguely embarrassing. An act favored by grandmothers who wore plain brown fringed shawls that they'd knitted themselves. If she wanted to pray, she realized, she would have to make it up.

In the corner of one shelf above her desk, she kept a small collection of little objects she'd found or been given over the years. They were piled together and forgotten; she hadn't looked at them for ages, yet they somehow still contained the aura of the sacred. Tiny talismans. She decided she would arrange them in a semicircle on the floor near her bed, and perhaps they would give her success when she spoke with her father. She wondered briefly if this were superstition instead of prayer. But she decided to recite a few words, and that, surely, would make it prayer.

First she selected a feather she'd found when she'd been walking with her father in the park three or four years ago. It was remarkably colored, white with tinges of violet. She'd intended to research to find out what kind of bird shed such a feather, but she hadn't done that yet. She put the feather on the floor not far from the head of her bed and squatted down. "Please, God," she said, and then she didn't know what to say next, so she rose and went back to her shelf. Next to the feather, she put a Chinese coin with a square cutout in the center that she'd bought in Chinatown. Then she added a brass bell Vic had given her. "Help me with my mother," she said before the three objects. She wasn't sure that was a prayer, but it was tangible. "And my father," she added after a minute.

She put two red candles in place next. Neither had been lit yet. She'd been saving them for a special occasion, and she realized this was that occasion, so she went out to the kitchen—past her mother's closed door—to get matches, and then to the bathroom to pull off two little squares of toilet paper. She put the toilet paper under each candle so that if they dripped, wax wouldn't get on the floor, and she thought it a good sign that she'd remembered that at all. Her mind was behaving, paying attention to details, and that would be important later when she spoke to her father.

As she lit the first candle, she murmured, "Sweet potato." As she lit the second, she said, "Pumpkin." She didn't know exactly why she said those words, but it occurred to her that it would soon be Thanksgiving, and she couldn't imagine Thanksgiving without her father living at home, so this had to be resolved before then.

She continued forming the semicircle with a tiny vial of topaz stones that had been in her Christmas stocking one year. Then two marbles, one a "jasper," white marbled with blue, and the other a "bloody," a red-black-and-white swirl. She placed them close together, as though they were a couple. She added a pinecone and said, "Sky" and then "Earth." Surely "sky" and "earth" were holy words. Next to the pinecone, she placed a little wooden frog, no larger than a muffin, with a ridged back that made a kind of music when rubbed with a stick stored in a hole that ran through its neck. She looked at the frog a few minutes, then took it away. Something about it struck her as unlucky for a prayer, though she couldn't say precisely why.

She wanted to finish soon because she wanted more sleep before dawn. She added a plastic bag full of chips of glimmering mica that she and Vic had collected on a family vacation to Arizona, and that was when she remembered poetry. Surely poetry was a prayer. Her father would agree with that. She went to the living room, straight to the built-in bookshelves that lined one wall and the two shelves where her father kept his favorite poetry books as well as those he'd edited. Mara didn't read much poetry. Math and science were more natural than words to her, which was another reason she needed help now. She ran her hand along the spines of the books, looking for one in particular. A slim Rilke volume, and a specific poem her father used to read to her. When she found it, she returned to her bedroom, stood in front of the candles and read.

"Praise the world to the angel, not the unutterable world;
you cannot astonish him with your glorious feelings;
in the universe, where he feels more sensitively, you're just a beginner.
Therefore, show him the simple thing that is shaped in passing. . . ."

There was more to the poem, but that was enough. Mara could almost see her father sitting in a rocking chair by this very bed, reading her that translation of that poem. "You're my little angel," he used to say, "the sensitive one." But what made Mara wonder was the idea that something could take its shape "in passing," as though it were an accident. If that were true, couldn't it be reshaped with relative ease? Was that what she needed to show her father?

The semicircle required one last item. Nothing left on her shelf seemed right, though admittedly she was operating on gut instinct instead of logic. She took her white school MetroCard and put it at the end of the arc. The perfect choice: a prayer, of sorts, to the subway, the subway that Aaron loved, the subway he'd once told her carried 4,800,000 commuters every weekday, the subway that separated her parents, one in Manhattan and the other in Brooklyn, and that would, if she were very, very lucky, allow her to reunite them.

NEW YORK: 5:53 A.M.
MECCA: 1:53 P.M.

It had been a long night of many moods. He'd packed a year of life into this night, Jonas thought. He'd been calm, then angry, then uncertain, then confident, then lost, then found. It had been an unpredictable night, a night, among other things, of great energy poured into written words.

The letters Jonas finished were fewer than he'd hoped, but they expressed exactly what he wanted to say. He decided he would not waste much time explaining. There would be questions about meaning and morality later, from those who loved him best as well as those who'd never known him. But he didn't want to create letters for intelligence operatives trying to untangle his motivation or, more likely, eager to label him disturbed or naive. These were personal letters: Vic's a poem of passion, his mother's an ode of gratitude.

For Vic, Jonas recalled that August day, the first time, when the rain finally finished and the tentative sun tiptoed onto the lake. Soon the pine trees cast longing shadows at the lake's edges. Its center reflected unselfconscious brilliance. And they emerged from the tent, first Vic, then Jonas, cautious but coupled. "I do not blame you for tiring of me," he wrote near the letter's end, "but I'll always be grateful for that day." For his mother, Jonas remembered winter afternoons and the warm kitchen, the two of them returned from a museum or a movie, sharing a late lunch of hot oatmeal with brown sugar melted on top, or miso soup, or noodles served in bowls she'd shaped and smoothed with her own hands, just as she'd shaped and smoothed him, her son. Then he apologized for not telling her the truth about NYU. "At first it was an accident that I didn't get my papers in on time. But I think it happened the way it was meant to," he wrote. He signed both letters identically: "Love and later, Jonas."

Just as he was about to slide his mother's letter into the envelope, he was struck with an image of her slumped at the kitchen table, taking on guilt, so he unfolded the letter and added a postscript. "I have not been brainwashed, Mom," he wrote. "I'm trying to prevent a larger destruction. I've struggled to understand the nature of our blood-stained world. I've had to look beyond simple definitions of 'good' and 'evil' and see symptoms in terms of their interconnectedness. This isn't your fault. You've been the best."

He wrote to Deirdre on the back of one of the two postcards he'd bought: "Check the news. I think you'll be proud of me. You were a lasting influence. Love, Jonas."

The physical act of writing pleased him as much as the notes' content. His hand moved across the page vigorously, and the marks he left there, some in cursive and some in schoolboy printing, seemed almost alive. Each letter's formation was fueled by a heave of anger he couldn't analyze, didn't even want to consider too deeply, but that seemed aimed at strangers who failed to understand the effects of their own actions. As he reached the end of his mother's letter, he felt his fury draining away. He felt himself slowing down to the point of molasses dripping from a tree in late autumn, or as if he were a child who has spent all morning in the playground, sliding and swinging and climbing so relentlessly that one act blends into the other, the monkey bars becoming the slide becoming the rope swing and so on, and who now, at last, is ready to nap.

This lull of weariness gave way to missing Vic again. By now his longing felt like a raw gape in his chest, yet his limbs were incongruously heavy. He couldn't escape it; he felt, too, an ache in his temples, the base of his neck, his groin. And it spread so that soon he also missed his father as well as his mother, and then, in varying degrees, neighbors and classmates and old girlfriends, especially Deirdre in Ireland, but also Heidi, with whom he'd shared a couple of weeks, and Else, his first awkward relationship, who he'd heard taught elementary school now. Then he missed other people who ambled through his brain almost randomly, some he'd known barely at all. Harold the Buddhist along with the man in the stained apron who'd made Jonas's final gyro. He thought of saying good-bye to them in his mind, one by one, but "good-bye" seemed a word that would kill him. The premature sense of loss paralyzed him.

Ritual. Ritual: a time-tested tool to deal with any transition, be it between day and night, fasting and eating, breathing and relinquishing breath. This was not the moment to invent a personal entreaty to Allah; he needed established practices, weighted by age-old customs, which would strengthen him and connect him with great spiritual traditions.

He began with the Islamic prayer ritual that he'd followed while training south of Peshawar. He went to the bathroom, lathered up the bar of soap, and went to work cleaning his hands. He lingered over the balls of his hands, each knuckle, the flesh between fingers, the skin above the nails, allowing his mind to be lulled with memories of Pakistan. He'd never been in that part of the world before, but he'd been eager when Masoud had suggested it. He flew to Islamabad, then took a train to Peshawar. There he was met by a taciturn man with a thin mustache that stretched across his face and pointed downward, like a persistent frown, who gave his name only as Ghalji and took Jonas to a madrassa, where they spent one night. Jonas was exhausted from the trip, the time difference, and nervousness. Yet he had trouble sleeping on the mat laid on the cement floor in a tiny room. He had just dozed when the call to predawn prayers came, and then he couldn't get back to sleep, so he was awake as boys began filing into the building early in the morning, some looking no older than five years old. All sat in neat rows on the floor of a large room, heavy Qur'ans on their laps, and as he peeked into the room, they glanced at him with either curiosity or animosity. Then Jonas heard yelling outside and went out to see a man on a bicycle shouting and gesturing as someone from the school, dressed identifiably all in white, stood shaking his head. Then Ghalji was standing next to Jonas, putting a hand on his arm, drawing him to the side. "What is it?" Jonas said, motioning with his head toward the man, who had now let his bicycle drop to the ground and seemed to be arguing and wailing at once.

"This man cannot find his son. He is blaming the school." Ghalji paused, then added, "But none of it concerns us. Are you ready?"

Jonas followed Ghalji to a jeep, and Ghalji drove past rice fields to a village called Darra Adam Khel. Jonas wrote the name down in a little notebook he'd brought with him. Now, scrubbing his arms to the elbows, Jonas recalled how awed he'd been by both the exoticism and the industriousness of the town's sole dirt street lined with gun-making shops, the sound of metal meeting metal that rose into the green mountains behind

Darra. He peeked into the slender rooms where gunsmiths dressed in *shalwar kameez* worked with primitive tools: pliers, hammers, small anvils. It felt like an adventure then, and he even forgot why he had come or how foreign he must look until he noticed the men lounging on rope beds who watched him with slitted eyes and murmured among themselves as he and Ghalji passed. He noticed, too, a boy wearing a turban as large as his own head and carrying an armload of oiled wood. The child stopped in the street's center to stare sullenly. Occasionally the sound of gunfire punched through the air as a gunsmith or potential customer tested the product. Jonas felt distinctly that he would be unsafe were he alone. Then it occurred to him to wonder what made him consider himself safe now, in the company of this unsmiling stranger. What if this were a setup? Wouldn't he be a prize to kidnap, dangle before the American people, and then behead? But he didn't think of this until he was already walking down the street, already without choice, and besides, he knew once he began disbelieving any part of what he was doing, the whole would fall apart.

"Few Westerners are permitted here," Ghalji said, as though guessing Jonas's thoughts. "Even despite our practice of *melmastia*." He'd already explained to Jonas about the region's famous commitment to hospitality. "But all our fighters are welcomed in Darra," he continued. "From here, they see our strength, and it builds their own confidence."

"Confidence," Jonas said aloud now to himself in the mirror, and then he started washing his mouth and nose. He could still vividly picture the shop he and Ghalji had entered near the street's end. Jonas trailed Ghalji into the back section, separated from the front by a curtain, and Ghalji gave him a fifteen-minute class in armaments. He showed Jonas guns made for long-range accuracy: .30-06-caliber rifles with intricate sights and long, tapered boat-tail bullets. He pointed out weapons made for power, like the .45-caliber Tommy Guns favored for years by Chicago gangsters and .50-caliber Browning machine guns that had to be mounted on vehicles. There were guns, too, for secrecy, some resembling pens or walking sticks or cigarette lighters or even cell phones, others modeled on the two-shot Derringer, compact enough to slide into a shoe.

"How many guns are here on this one street?" Jonas asked.

"They produce perhaps seven hundred every day," Ghalji said. "But they sell as quickly as they are made."

When they left, two armed men from Darra accompanied them, riding in the back of the jeep. Jonas asked no questions. They drove in the direction of Afghanistan, following a stony pass that ran beside several crumbled buildings. Ghalji interrupted the silence to tell him they were in a tribal area now, well beyond the rule of the Pakistani government or its army or its laws. Jonas made no comment. After perhaps thirty minutes, Ghalji parked the jeep and they traveled the last mile or so on foot, following a path so discreet that Jonas could not have retraced his steps alone.

Jonas started in now on washing his feet and toes, beginning on the right one. This was the end of the ritual that he had carried out three times each day at the Pakistani camp. He lived in a cement barracks with twenty-seven other men, including some who'd been there for more than a year. There were others, Pakistani ISI officers, Ghalji told him, and one German engineer. All of them ate together, simple meals consisting mainly of chapati and lentils. Ghalji stayed with Jonas, serving as interpreter and guide but never for a second becoming personable.

Despite that, Jonas felt far less isolated than he had back home. He felt part of something larger than himself. En masse, they rose each morning and prayed. Together in the evenings, they listened to what Jonas would call motivational lectures, sermons about the evil of the West, America in particular, and the virtues of jihad. Ghalji insisted Jonas attend and sat next to him, whispering a translation of each lecture in his ear. After the first couple of days, however, Jonas began to allow his mind to wander. It wasn't only that the message struck him as simplistic. By that time of day, he was tired. In between the morning prayers and the evening lectures, they engaged each day in a nonstop variety of strenuous physical exercises and drills. Some days they trained with machine guns, firing weapons made in Darra as they hung from ropes or ran through obstacles. Some days they target-practiced with rocket-propelled grenades. For four days, Jonas and five other men were taken aside and given special training related to suicide bombing missions. They were taught how to handle delicate explosives made from hydrogen peroxide and nail-polish remover. They were instructed on methods to avoid suspicion, how to disguise the presence of the explosives on their bodies, what to do if they were stopped for questioning on their way to a mis-sion, and how and when to use a detonator. Jonas did not yet know anything about November 9 and New York City, so the lessons had still seemed so—scrubbing himself in the bathroom, he hunted for the right word—so *remote*. Like learning the Heimlich maneuver in a high school PE class.

Cleansed now, Jonas stood at the end of the prayer mat, tried to clear his mind, and then raised both arms and began the first *rak'a*. "Allah is most great." He crossed his arms over his chest and bent at the waist and continued with the series of motions and gestures and words he'd been taught, prostrating himself and then rising to repeat it.

When he finished, he touched his chest. The sting of anxiety felt different, perhaps, but not improved. Instead of radiating through his body, it had become a spasm convulsing in a painfully compacted region squeezed between his lungs.

A smorgasbord of sacraments, then. He had to ease the paroxysm, so that was what he would try. He felt himself Muslim as much as Jewish, as much as Buddhist, or Christian, or Hindu, and he needed, now, their joint power.

He sat cross-legged on the prayer mat, rotated his shoulders a few times, and began to meditate, clearing his mind by thinking "so" on each inhale and "hum" on each exhale. He did it for as long as he could, clearing his mind repeatedly. Then he recited a mantra aloud: *"Om mani padme hum. Om mani padme hum."* He used his prayer beads to count, running them through his fingers loosely as he recited the mantra ninety times. Next he lit a smudge stick he'd brought in his backpack, a bundle of dried sage. He fanned the swirls of smoke around his feet, then his waist, and finally his head. He circled the room's perimeter, smudge stick in hand, paying special attention to the wall connecting him to the subway's underground life, the wall that vibrated with passing trains. Soon the scents of the Southwestern desert filled the studio apartment off the Avenue of the Finest. He extinguished the smoldering herb bundle in the bathtub.

It occurred to him that his behavior might be considered disturbed. Bordering on the obsessive. If he were being spied on through a keyhole, he imagined at this point Masoud would break in again and tell him simply that he was unfit to carry out the martyrdom. But he knew he was fit for *that* moment. The anguish of *this* one tormented him.

He turned, finally, to the religion of his father. He took a pot from the kitchen, filled it with water, and began *negal vasser*, the traditional morning ritual washing of one's hands three times, starting with the right hand. The purpose, as he'd been taught, was to cleanse oneself from the dust of death that attached to a person as he slept, and thus to achieve *tumah*, the Hebrew word for purification.

He scrubbed more vigorously than before, so forcefully that he felt his left arm grow hot as his right hand rubbed it. It was as if he were trying to stimulate the flow of blood through the veins to cleanse his inner organs, as if he were massaging the muscles themselves. As he rinsed his hands for the third time, his skin stiffening from the cold water and the repeated friction, he realized his loneliness had intensified with each ritual. He stopped then. He stopped and dried himself and sat cross-legged on the floor so he could look out the window and see the night that was beginning to switch from black to gray. Morning. His last.

Was he scared? Yes, he was. But when he broke it down, the largest part of what scared him was that he would fail. And then he would be arrested and tried, and his effort would become a joke instead of a sincere attempt to wake people up, to make them face the arrogant violence of their own country, the killing and maiming and torturing that had to end. Words had become as ineffectual in his country as the lectures parents gave their teenagers. Action was required. Of this he felt certain. It was harder to envision what lay ahead for him personally. What separation, what joining. Even though Masoud's model of afterlife didn't ring true for Jonas, to go from this vibrancy to nothingness seemed improbable. Too cruel. Being in limbo also seemed an unhappy prospect.

Jonas thought, then, of the dialogue group he'd once attended: New Yorkers gathered to share near-death experiences. A friend had invited him, a man in one of his meditation classes. The group met in an apartment on the Upper East Side, maybe seventy people crowded into two rooms, and everyone, it turned out, wanted to talk. The experiences, recited one after the other, were remarkably similar and by now wildly familiar:

the sensation of floating above one's body, moving down a tunnel toward light, being bathed in bliss, experiencing a panoramic life review. Perhaps by now, Jonas thought, everyone had heard of these sensations so often that they were programmed to remember those stories as their own.

A scientist who'd had his own near-death moments when he'd fallen down a mountainside in the Italian Alps was among those gathered, and someone in the group asked him if there might be a physical explanation for the shared near-death phenomena. Jonas leaned forward in his seat as the man spoke, using expressions like "neuro-physiological factors" and "stimulation of the temporal lobe." He talked of the possibility that certain chemicals bounced off a part of the brain and activated neurons, creating the commonly reported near-death sensations. The scientist finished by saying that research remained inconclusive, but he personally thought it most likely that love and light were simply typical elements encountered on the path between what he called, genially and neutrally, "here and there."

Here and there. Love and light. Jonas tried to sedate himself with those thoughts. He lay back on the red bedspread and encouraged his shoulders to unclench. He tried to drain his mind of nostalgia. He tried to imagine himself as light and love, sacred, devoted, exploding.

Jake awoke to the sound of Carol's calm, steady voice seeping from the kitchen, where she was speaking on the telephone. It filled him with optimism: they would find Jonas today; they would resolve this; it would, in the end, be understood as a typical parenting trial. Carol had closed the door to the living room, so it was a muted version of her words and intonations that slipped through the crack between the door and the wall, falling into his ears. Hearing that, waking up in her presence—well, more or less in her presence—and feeling more secure about Jonas, he found himself swallowed by a wave of nostalgia and longing.

Sometimes Jake still felt himself to be a teenager in his cravings. He wasn't proud of this; he simply observed it. He still had the teenager's desire to dive headlong into a rush of reckless intimacy that would, each time, surprise him with its inventions and awe him by its intensity. He loved the vibrations that radiated from his center out to his fingertips, and he loved the sense that something was being revealed to him, another curtain pulled back for this boy from Ohio who as a child had been so loved, yes, and so sheltered.

But he was changing. Here he was, after all, fifty-two. *So, finally*. He could almost hear Carol, laughter floating beneath her words. *You're growing up, old man.*

Yes, okay, I see my own mortality now. I can start to see the arc of my own life. But, old man? I still want romance at the edge of a lake, or with candles lit late when it feels like no one else in the world is awake.

What he wanted was probably impossible: freshness and imagination and exhilaration, but now he wanted it coupled with reliability and serenity. If any of his relationships had the possibility of embodying it, it was the one with Carol, except, of course, that relationship had long gone cold. Until now.

The kitchen, he realized, had fallen silent. She was off the telephone. So he rose, ran his fingers through his hair, and pushed open the door that separated them. She sat at the kitchen table, her head in her hands. A pen and paper lay next to her; she'd been doodling. She'd always doodled when she was worried. Even now, he remembered those kinds of details about Carol.

He squeezed her shoulder once, not wanting to overstep the boundary that she'd built between them, that he knew he'd caused her to build. "It's going to be okay. You want a cup of coffee?" he asked. She didn't answer, so he went to the cabinet and opened the door that held the can of coffee.

"Jake."

He turned to her. She'd raised her head now. "Everything," she said. Her hands were both lying palm-down on the table, fingers spread. "Everything gets lost so easily." Her eyes were wide and very silent. Her body, too, was completely motionless, but the muscles in her arms looked strained, as though keeping them immobile required enormous effort.

"What?"

"And there's too much to understand. The world's too big, and the Internet makes it seem like we're connected, but we aren't really. We can't possibly understand."

"Carol," he said, "what are you talking about?"

"I have something to tell you. Last night, before you got here, I called the police."

Jake felt a rush of irritation that surprised him with its force. Must be he still had an ingrained suspicion of cops, stemming from nothing more than his pot-smoking days. The days when cops, even those his age, had seemed like the staid, corrupt establishment. Carol responded to the objections written on his face before he could speak.

"I had to," she said. "I'm scared, Jake, and I couldn't hold myself back any longer. I told them it might be premature. They put me on with this detective, very nice, who sounded soothing and said to call him again if Jonas didn't show up in twenty-four hours."

Jake nodded. "Our original plan anyway." He poured a potful of water into the coffeemaker.

"But after you told me about the airline ticket, I called back again."

"Last night?"

She nodded. "The detective wasn't there anymore. So I told the officer who answered about Jonas and Pakistan, and I gave him the detective's name, and they put me on hold for five minutes and then they patched me through to the guy's cell phone or his home or something, and I told him."

Jake turned to the counter and scooped some coffee grains into a filter, aware of his sense of optimism draining away, trying to resist its loss. "We still need to give it today, Carol," he said.

"He just called back," Carol said.

Jake flipped on the coffeemaker. He sat down across from Carol.

"It turns out the man's name . . ."

"What man?"

"Jonas's friend from the class. His name is Masoud . . ." She glanced at a paper resting under her elbow. "Masoud al-Zufak. Or close enough. Anyway, the name means something to them. The detective didn't say, exactly, but they're interested in the guy; that much is clear."

"Hell, they're interested in anyone with an Arab-sounding name," Jake said. "That doesn't convict him of anything."

"The detective listed these characteristics . . ." She trailed off.

"Characteristics?"

"Profile, he said, of a homegrown terrorist."

"What? They are *already* accusing this guy Masoud—"

"Not Masoud, Jake," she said. "Jonas."

"What?"

"Or at least, people who get talked into things, which is what he thinks Jonas is. He was describing the personality type. Often naive, he said. From a liberal background."

"Oh, yeah. It's so fucking dangerous to be liberal."

"Just listen. Seeking to fill a void. Distressed or angry about something they believe to be unjust."

"What the hell are you getting at?"

"The detective is getting a warrant, Jake. He wanted to let me know. He's going to search Jonas's apartment. This morning."

"Jesus. This isn't making sense."

"I know. I know, it's like a foreign language, but—you remember that Christmas Eve, years ago, when I was robbed?"

He remembered. It had been after midnight, and she'd headed home from a friend's apartment. They had so little money in those days, certainly not enough for a taxi, and yet it didn't matter. They were two bohemians, living their way. She took the bus and walked down the dark street to their apartment. She was jumped. Two guys and a girl. They wanted cash, and she didn't have any. She was saved by a neighbor who'd just returned from a party and came rushing out his front door when he heard her scream. He shouted, and the muggers ran. The neighbor walked her home. And when she arrived and told Jake, he felt his own knees weaken.

"My God, I could have lost you," he'd said, pulling her into his arms.

It was as if all the moments he'd unconsciously avoided thinking about were flooding him, an abundance of memories, one leading to another and another.

"Yes, I remember," he said now.

"The cops were barely attentive," she said, her words indicating that she wasn't remembering the same moments Jake did. "*Another mugging. Big deal*. That was their attitude."

"Times are different," Jake said, doubting himself that the cliché applied when it came to the police.

"They've jumped all over this, Jake. They aren't treating it like some case of a mom overreacting. They want a list of Jonas's friends. They want to question you. This morning. They asked to come here. Something's happening."

Jake got up. He poured them both cups of coffee, adding a splash of milk to hers. Then he hit his fist on the counter, surprised by his own ferocity. "Goddamn it, Carol. Jonas is not a fucking terrorist. And I don't want to talk to anyone who thinks he is."

"They're on their way."

"I thought we were going to go back to his apartment to look for clues. Try to locate friends we didn't know about."

"They're doing that."

"What if," he said, and let those two words sit there for a moment. "What if my girlfriend theory is right or Jonas has just been busy or even if he's in the throes of some late-adolescent rebellion and doesn't want to talk with us?"

"I know." She took a sip of her coffee. "It's so hard to know your kids at this age. He'll be so pissed at me if this is all getting out of hand." She reached out and touched his arm. "Let it be getting out of hand. But that detective's response," she pulled back, "it scares me more than anything else."

Jake, too, felt long tendrils of fear in his stomach, like a foot of thick rope being pulled from his throat through his chest and stomach, down toward his feet. He sat down across from her and took a deep breath. "If you're right, and something is very wrong, do we want to trust the cops to handle it? I don't know, Carol. This is our son. Shouldn't *we* talk to his friends? Shouldn't *we* call this center where he took the class and see if we can find out anything more instead of sitting here answering questions while cops write down stuff we already know?"

"Oh, Jake." Carol pressed her hand against her mouth as if holding back words for a moment, then made a fist. "I don't know what to do." Her eyes became slightly glazed. "He's the best of both of us. He learns while he sleeps; we used to tell him that, remember? And he's passionate and moral and there's this quiet streak that runs through him and that always calmed me. If he thinks he's doing the right thing, nothing can stop him. But he also gets depressed. He feels like something's missing, like the world is immoral and only he sees it." Carol met Jake's eyes. "All I know is I keep getting the feeling Jonas is in trouble. He's in trouble and we need to reach him, and we need all the help we can get."

Jake stared into his cup and then drank the last of the coffee in it. "Okay," he said, and he rose from the table and squeezed her shoulder. "Okay, I'll talk to the goddamn cops."

"Good," she said as they heard the buzzer. "Because here they are."

Mara overslept. She overslept badly, and she knew it the moment she awoke. She didn't stop to decipher what finally made her stir, whether external clatter like a car alarm or some shudder from within. She just jumped out of bed with her eyes barely open, kicked over the bell she'd set on the floor the night before, glanced at the clock to confirm her fears, tugged on a pair of pants, tucked in her nightshirt, and pulled a sweatshirt over her head. She slipped on her boots without socks, grabbed her coat, stuck the chosen rocks in her pocket, started out of the room, remembered the MetroCard on the floor, and returned to get it. She rushed past her mother's door—closed, as usual.

Outside the apartment, Aaron was slumped down on the floor, leaning against the wall, his head resting on his backpack. He wore his coat, unzipped. As she stepped into the hallway, he opened his eyes and began to rise.

"I'm so sorry," Mara whispered because she didn't want to wake her mom, and then she closed the door as quietly as she could, turning the handle first. "Let's go."

She led the way to the elevator, and Aaron followed. He followed as she walked out the building, down the street, and around the corner to the subway station. Before she reached the stairs, she slowed and turned to talk to Aaron, but she weighed too little to anchor herself and felt herself being gently carried forward through the narrowing of foot traffic at the subway entrance, her toes grazing the ground, making contact and then losing it the way they might if she were bobbing in a swimming pool. She moved in this fashion until she reached the foot of the stairs, and then she managed to expel herself from the pre-rush-hour flow of work-bound commuters and press her back against the wall. There she waited. Aaron saw her and steered himself in her direction. She took his hand. They held hands until they got to the turnstile, and then they separated to slide their cards separately through the machine.

"This way," Aaron said, heading toward the downtown B-train, and then he cocked his head and said, "One's coming," so they rushed down the stairs and arrived just in time to get on the B, the recorded admonition, "Stand clear of the closing doors," ringing out behind them. Standing room only. They found a place in the corner.

"Were you waiting there since six?" Mara asked as the subway screeched to a start.

Aaron nodded.

"You didn't think I'd changed my mind?"

Aaron looked surprised. "No. I thought you'd overslept."

"And you are still okay with this?"

He nodded again.

A woman was smiling at them. A man sitting next to her rose and spoke to Mara. "Would you like my seat?"

Mara shook her head, but Aaron said, "Sit," and the man added, "Please," so Mara did. She scooted over so Aaron could squeeze in next to her. They didn't talk for a few stops. It was still early, and everyone in the car was quiet. A few people read magazines or listened to music on earphones. No one spoke. Then Aaron leaned close to Mara. "Is your dad still going to be there?" he asked quietly. "For sure?"

This was the question that Mara had been refusing to consider. Her father's office hours had never been absolute. Sometimes, in the past, he'd left the house at 7 o'clock in the morning, sometimes he'd stayed home until 2 or 3 in the afternoon, editing in the apartment and then going to the office. But she didn't want to share her uncertainty with Aaron. She needed his confidence in her.

"He'll be there," she said. "I'll call as soon as we're in the neighborhood."

The subway emerged aboveground to carry them over the Manhattan Bridge. Aaron stood to look out the window, and Mara joined him. She'd never taken the B this far before. Out the window, she saw graffiti scrawled on the roof of

Chinatown buildings, tags in spray paint like "Cake87" and "Skidman." Also, a boat trail like a ribbon on the Hudson River, and the silver skyline of Manhattan, looking shiny and fresh. It seemed much prettier from a distance than it did up close, and she wondered briefly if that might be how it was with everything.

They changed at the Pacific/Atlantic stop. Mara stayed close to Aaron as they went down one set of stairs and up another to catch the next train. The number 4 was less crowded. A panhandler started at one end—she could hear him giving his spiel: "If you ain't got it, I understand, 'cause I ain't got it. But if you can spare . . ." He shuffled through the car. He paused in front of Mara, a look on his face that was puzzled and pained at once. She thought he must be waiting for her to give him some money, so she dug in her coat pocket, searching a little helplessly for change, but he just shook his head, said, "God bless, child," and, after a moment, walked on.

They got off at Utica, the train's last stop. Aboveground, it felt colder than Manhattan to Mara, though that seemed unlikely. At the corner, a stall selling homemade Caribbean-style chicken was already doing business. Next door, a beauty-salon window was decorated with three pictures of black women, each with different hairstyles, that looked like they had been torn from maga-zines and taped up from the inside. The streets were busy, but Mara did not see any children. Some passersby eyed Mara and Aaron with open curiosity. Mara felt conspicuous, and, looking at Aaron, she could see he did, too.

Aaron reached into his pocket, pulling out a map that he'd printed out from the computer. "This way," he said. They walked two blocks in one direction and three in another. At the corner, he pointed to the street sign.

"St. Johns and Kingston," she said, grinning at him. "What time is it?"

Aaron wore a wrist-watch, something else that set him apart from Mara's other classmates. "A little after eight."

She wanted to get out of the wind to call her father. "C'mon." She took Aaron's hand and pulled him into a small deli.

The man behind the counter was selling a pack of cigarettes to a customer, but he paused as they entered. "You kids need some help?"

"Can I stand here to make a call?"

The man eyed Mara and Aaron for a long beat before answering, "Sure."

Mara dialed her father's new home number and let it ring. No answer. The store had only two aisles, and Aaron began walking down one of them, inspecting the shelves. "I'm going to try his cell," she said.

Her father answered on the second ring. Mara felt relief shoot up her spine.

"Mara." He sounded angry. "Are you at school?"

"No," she said. "School doesn't start until 8:40."

"Then where the—?"

"I'm here," she said.

"What do you mean *here?*"

"St. Johns and Kingston," she said. "I'm at the corner."

"What? How did you get there?"

"Subway. And now we're in a deli."

"No deli," corrected the man behind the counter. "De-Morris Bodega."

"De-Morris Bodega," Mara repeated. "Can you come meet us?"

"The subway? Alone? Mara, you know—"

"I'm with Aaron," she interrupted.

"Aaron?" Her father sounded incredulous. "Does his mother—"

"Dad, can you just come meet us?"

"You scared us, Mara. Damn. I've been calling everyone."

"Dad."

Her father let out a breath of impatient air. "I'm not there."

Mara looked around guiltily. Aaron, still among the shelves about ten steps away, glanced over at her. She didn't want him to know, not yet. She tried to speak quietly. "Where are you? How soon can you get here?"

"I'm here. I'm . . . I'm at home."

Though her father spoke hesitantly and sounded confused, Mara was not. She suddenly saw with sharp clarity that prayer was a powerful tool. Her father had returned home. "Good," she said. "Home."

"I came to . . . to talk with you. I thought we could have breakfast together. Both your mother and I were surprised to find you gone. And we're going to have to discuss your actions, Mara."

"You're moving back," Mara said, barely hearing the rest of it. "He's moving back," she said to Aaron, who was closer now and watching her.

"Mara. No."

"You're not?"

"I wanted to talk with you over breakfast. I wanted to hear how things are going for you. School. Other stuff."

"School?" Now she felt confused.

"Let's save it for in person," her father said. "Look, put Aaron on for a minute."

Mara walked back to Aaron, who was standing in an aisle looking at a box labeled "Jamaican-style dough mix." She handed him the phone.

"Hello?" Aaron said. "Yes, sir . . . yes . . . okay . . . okay, 'bye." He handed the phone back to Mara.

"You two walk right back to the subway," her father said. "It's, let's see . . . it's about 8:05. You should be here by 9:25. I'm going to meet you at the station—I'll be waiting there by 9:15, so call me as soon as you're aboveground, okay?"

"Okay, but, Dad—"

"Just get back here, Mara. Then we'll talk. I promise we'll talk for as long as it takes. We can all be a little late today," her father said.

Mara hung up the phone and looked at Aaron, who had gone back to inspecting the food.

"I don't understand," she said. "But maybe it's good—I mean, he's home and he wants . . ." She trailed off, suddenly noticing that Aaron was holding a jar of something called "Horlicks breakfast drink" and appeared to be intently reading the ingredients. She began to dig in her coat pocket. "You didn't have any breakfast, did you?"

Aaron shrugged and put down the jar.

"Let's get something."

"Your dad said we should go right away," Aaron said.

"We will. But . . ." She approached the man behind the counter. "What can you recommend for breakfast?"

The man grinned at her. He pointed to what looked like slices of pound cake, individually wrapped. "Coconut sweetbread, missy," he said.

Mara dug in her pocket in earnest and pulled out seventy-eight cents. "How much for two slices?" she asked.

"Two dollars."

"I have five dollars," said Aaron.

"But I want to treat you. You got up early and you came all this way and—"

"It's okay. If I hadn't come, what would I have been doing? Just sleeping."

Aaron said it so seriously that she laughed, and then he pulled out his money and she added her coins and they left with the coconut sweetbread, which they began eating as they walked back to the subway.

It was still cold and the sky looked thick, but just as they reached the subway station, the sun seemed to muscle aside the clouds for a minute. A ray of sunshine fell on Mara's shoulders. She looked at the street behind them, the rush of life, and she thought perhaps she understood what her father meant by "authentic." In fact, this might be the solution. It seemed a stroke of brilliance, and she didn't know why she hadn't thought of it before. Mara and her mother should move to this neighborhood and live here with her father. She would discuss it with her dad. Maybe it was even what he planned to propose. Yes, that was probably it. This realization made her so excited that she reached over and hugged Aaron, and giggled at the startled expression on his face, and took his hand, and together they dipped down the stairs into the subway, leaving the sunshine behind.

Vic stood in the bathroom, waiting for the water running in the sink to warm up. She wasn't going to worry, not yet, but she hoped her father would call back soon. It had been half an hour since he'd rung to tell her Mara was missing. She knew there had to be a reasonable explanation, probably something to do with school. Vic had always been the one to pull stupid stunts; Mara was reliability personified. Still, Vic had carried the receiver with her into the bathroom, setting it on the toilet so she wouldn't miss her father's call.

The dream she'd been having when the phone woke her was of tomorrow's opening night. Not the performance so much, though she had dreamt of a stage lit with such force that shadows feared, an audience hushed in anticipation, her kicks precise, her body arcing as smoothly as the letter C. Most of the dream, though, had been of Jonas in the theater, smiling, and then Jonas at dinner afterward, the two of them in some dimly lit café, their fingers touching, the food unimportant, but nevertheless she dreamt of a bowl of kalamata olives and a plate with cubes of feta cheese, and wherever he had been and whyever he hadn't called now explained and behind them. She dreamt of herself struggling to express something intangible, and him understanding at once, reaching to embrace her.

She glanced at the clock and pulled her hair back so she could wash her face. Out of nowhere conscious, she flashed on an image of Mara—a memory from last winter, when the two of them had made New York City–style s' mores, roasting the marshmallows over the kitchen burner using a rosewood-handled stainless-steel kebab skewer and then slapping them between graham crackers and chocolate and warming the whole concoction in the microwave for five seconds. She remembered Mara, her face glowing with an orangeish light from the flames, telling a joke—a knock-knock joke, something silly, what had it been? "Knock, knock." "Who's there?" "Zeke." "Zeke who?" "Zeke and you shall find." And they'd both started giggling, Vic pleased to see Mara acting like a kid. Vic thought now that was the last time she could remember seeing Mara laugh.

She was drying her face when the phone rang again. She picked it up. "Did you find her?" she asked.

"Vic? It's Carol."

"Who?"

"Jonas's mom."

"Oh," she said. "I'm sorry—my sister—well, anyway, hi."

"Everything okay? I hope it's not too early?"

"No, no, everything's fine."

"You haven't heard from Jonas?"

Vic sank right onto the bathroom rug, her legs crossed. "No."

"I knew you'd call me . . . but I wanted to check. You see, Jonas's dad and I, we've decided to contact the police."

"Police?" Vic realized she'd stopped breathing.

"We found out he went to Pakistan in September. Do you know about that?"

"Pakistan? Jonas?" Vic said. "No. It was a yoga retreat."

"The police would like to speak with you," Jonas's mother said.

"Police?"

"Since you are one of his closest—well, probably his closest . . ." Her voice faltered for a moment. "And because of the Pakistan trip, I was wondering about friends he might have discussed that with, and I thought of this man he mentioned once or twice. I think he's from Saudi Arabia. I don't know if you know him?"

"I do," Vic said. "Masoud. I know him."

"Masoud. Good. And his last name? Do you happen to know it?"

"Al-Zufak," Vic said slowly.

Jonas's mother exhaled, as though a lakeful of air was coming out of her, and that was how Vic recognized how tightly she was wound. "Masoud al-Zufak," she repeated, but not directly into the phone receiver, as if she were relaying the name to

258

someone else in the room. "Zu-fak," she pronounced again, and then, after a pause, "Vic, do you have contact information?"

"No, but he—" Vic was going to mention last night's odd phone call but stopped herself. Masoud was Jonas's friend. She didn't want to see him get in any trouble. These were times of appalling biases, when anyone from an Arab country could be dragged into custody for sneezing.

"What? Vic, anything is helpful," Jonas's mother said.

"I . . . I was just going to say . . . I think he lives somewhere in Brooklyn."

"Brooklyn. Thank you."

"But you know . . . Masoud really likes Jonas. I'm sure he'd want to do anything he could to help you."

"Yes, I'm sure you're right," Jonas's mother said, though in a distracted way. "Jonas also liked—likes—Masoud. But this is the way they want to do it." Vic heard a noise like something dropping in the background from wherever Jonas's mother was. "Whatever will help us find Jonas is what I want," she said. "You understand?"

"Yeah. Sure."

"And finding this Masoud may help us find Jonas."

"This Masoud." It was such a distancing way to express it. There it was again: the "they" that became an "us" and that was separate from this Arab man considered suspicious simply because of his name. That was something Vic did not want to be part of. "Are you . . . are you sure Jonas is missing?" Even as Vic asked it, she knew on some intuitive level that this was it precisely. Jonas was missing. Whatever "missing" meant. Maybe he'd been hit by a car or lost his memory or been kidnapped by criminals. Otherwise he would have called her. He *would* have. How could she have thought anything else for even a second? Jonas would have called Vic by now if he could. A chill swept from the soles of her feet to her stomach. She felt her shoulders clench.

"So. The police will be in touch with you. They say they'll send someone to interview you."

Vic felt her heart in her neck. "Okay," she said softly.

"Thanks, Vic. I'm sorry. We'll . . . we'll probably laugh about this someday," Jonas's mother said. "I just want to get to that day, you know?" Then the phone line went dead.

Jonas missing. Vic dialed his cell phone one more time and got his voice mail. "Shit, Jonas. You are scaring us all. Call me, damnit. Call me, call me," she said, like a prayer, and then she hung up.

She was pulling on a pair of jeans when her home phone rang again. "Hello?" she said, thinking, *Jonas, Jonas, Jonas*.

"Vic, it's okay." It was her father. Vic had forgotten about Mara being gone.

"Oh, Dad," she said.

"She and Aaron went to Brooklyn, can you believe that? To try to find me. I don't know where she got that idea; she doesn't even know my address. But anyway, I just spoke with her and they promised to hop right back on that subway. She should be here by 9:30, and we'll have breakfast. I figure she can skip morning classes today, and I've let them know at the office that I'll be late."

Vic's father sounded like he wanted her to realize he was making an effort; he wanted her approval. But Vic was thinking of something else. She remembered now Mara's plan to talk to their father, and she felt ashamed that she hadn't remembered it earlier, or asked Mara about it on the phone last night. "Oh, God," she said.

"Okay, baby. Sorry to have alarmed you for nothing," her father said. "I'll talk to you before your opening tomorrow night, okay?"

Vic wasn't listening. "God—Mara. But she's fine, right?"

"Completely."

"So that means maybe . . ."

"What?"

"Nothing. Just . . . maybe we'll find other missing people."

"Vic. What are you talking about?"

"Jonas," she said.

"Jonas? Where's he gotten himself to?" Her father sounded slightly amused now.

"We don't know, but his parents are freaking."

Vic's father laughed. "Well, a young man. That's a different matter than a little girl."

"Yes, but—"

"He'll turn up, Vic."

Vic closed her eyes and imagined Jonas's face, his blue eyes, his hair. "Yes. Maybe so." But her father had already replaced the receiver.

Underground at Columbus Circle, three lanky boys wearing do-rags were setting up their "orchestra," a couple African *djembe* drums along with some homemade cans—a metal sink, a plastic tub overturned, two wide pipes—as Sonny ambled by. Despite a night of evil dreams that had left Sonny queasy, a morning pang of hunger had kicked in, and he'd dragged himself up into the station. The Columbus Circle station was God's heaven, far as the trash cans went. Everything in the neighborhood, from a cuppa on up, was too costly—so, as proof of the perversity of human nature, folks stopped valuing it. They took a bite or two and then let it go, and the food they tossed aside at Columbus Circle on any given morning was enough to keep Sonny full for half the day; he could eat and not worry for dinner.

He'd finished a successful round of trash-can-hopping: a banana with one little bruise, a quarter of a croissant, almost all of a turkey sandwich on rye with Dijon, even a half-bottle of aspirin he planned to give Mrs. Wu next time he saw her. He ate until he felt refreshed and ready to go to work—just in time for rush hour. Then he spotted the three musicians. They were silent as they prepared to perform but looked rhythmic even without music, the lines of their legs and arms rotating around the curves of the drums as they pulled the instruments into a half-circle. The sight of them, so out-of-season hopeful, moved him. Despite the late-autumn cold, despite the Monday-morning commuter fog, these boys stood ready to remind their passing audience that even on the saddest, most frigid of days, there was much to relish in this world. They looked lucky, too; some kind of sheen on their cheeks gave them that. Sonny had been seeing so many people who didn't look lucky lately that the three of them went a ways toward improving his mood. He inched a little closer, feeling better than if it were Christmas. Not that that was any comparison; in this most plentiful of lands, Christmas had become a holiday of failures sorrowful enough to sink all the way down into the subway. Point being, these boys made him feel, as his momma would say, like the dawn of the Second Coming. As though with their music, the only tears from now on would be of gratification.

The musicians were nearly set up when one of them, the largest, put out a hat to collect the hand-outs. Sonny reached into his pocket and dropped in fifty cents.

The drummer laughed. "We ain't even started playing yet, old man."

"Just the same," Sonny said. "This morning I got it, so I can share it."

He nodded and began to shuffle away, deciding to try his luck for a while on the D-train. He would head uptown for four or five stops, then reverse his order. Stay central for the morning, maybe head back into Brooklyn after lunchtime.

"Wait, brother," one of the musicians called. Sonny noticed, when he turned, that the speaker had a small tattoo of an eagle on the right side of his neck. "You paid," he said. "Now let us play one for you."

Truth be told, Sonny desired no further extension of his workday break, but another minute or two wouldn't hurt. "You gonna want more of my money afterward?" he asked, smiling, and they laughed with him.

"Nah. Just get us an audience started, brother," the musician said as he took his place between the other two. He seemed to go quiet inside for a second and then began bouncing his chin in time to some internal rhythm. After a few seconds, the center drummer glanced at his band-mates and they began playing, the one on the right using sticks on both the sink and the pipe, the other two with their palms on the drums, hands traveling fast enough to blur, their music a story without words, a new ancient rhythm raising Sonny's spirit even higher and setting one foot tapping.

A memory rose in him then. Ruby and he, along with their momma, at church on Sunday. He'd never wanted to go; to his way of thinking,

Sunday wasn't intended for church. It was meant for a pancake breakfast or a mean game of street baseball or, later on, recovering from Saturday night. But church, Momma used to tell him, was his Hobson's choice, meaning it was no choice at all. As long as he lived in her house, to his memory, he'd missed only half-a-dozen church Sundays, and then only when he convinced Momma he felt sick enough that her dragging him out of bed would be a larger sin than him failing to walk through those holy doors.

No matter how many times they changed apartments, Momma kept them going to the same church—a bitty one squeezed between a nail salon and Derrell's Jerk Chicken Den, nothing from the outside to show it was even a church except for the green sign: Howard Street's Holy Home of Jesus. Didn't matter the season, the women all wore dresses the color of Easter eggs. And the music—that was what carried him from this moment back to that one. No drums made of sinks, of course, but there were always drums of some sort, along with a piano, a horn, sometimes something else if someone brought it. That music was a letting down of all the reservations that kept one body separate from another. The children would begin bouncing in their folding chairs at the first note, and soon enough one grown-up and then another would rise, the women starting to sway, the men beating on their own legs, and at the front of the room there'd be three or four women singing as if it were the last thing they'd ever do. And after that music, so powerful it made your blood beat in time, folks in turn would leap to their feet and begin to exclaim, the details of their week viewed through the prism of God and punctuated with "Save the Lord," each detail answered with "Yes, brother. Amen," the Rev. Herbert Watkis calling out, singing out encouragement, "Don't you run *away* from God if you done something wrong. Run straight *into* his arms and all your sins *are* forgiven," and everything, the musical confessions and pardons, the undulating hips and jumping feet, was a dance that carried them to some ecstasy beyond themselves. Momma always left those services feeling so much better, but it occurred to Sonny that it wasn't the Lord so much as the music and the folks that deserved the credit.

In some way, Sonny thought, the subway was his church. A holy, sanctified place of worship. There wasn't a single preacher; the homily was delivered by a mix of voices, the gospel sung beneath the sermon. And now the congregation was beginning to gather before these three musicians, four or five folks pausing, not too many 'cause most were rushing to day jobs, matters of the flesh, as it were, but it was fine—wherever two or more of us be gathered in His name—and even those hurrying by would on occasion throw a smile over their shoulders or pause long enough to reach into a pocket and drop a couple of coins into the hat. Remembering, for a second, Thine Amazing Grace.

Even as the three were drumming, gospel lyrics began wandering through Sonny's head, as though the drumming had unhinged the words from their songs and was mixing them together as randomly as subway commuters themselves are mixed—"Strongest trials, my heavenly spirit. Loudly sings saved a wretch like me. How sweet the infinite sake of the Lord, they fade and decay."

It occurred to Sonny that if this could be considered his church, then he might say he'd turned out to be just as devout as his momma always was. Which would have surprised her some. He'd explain his way of thinking to Ruby next time he saw her. She'd at least get a laugh out of the idea, and maybe she'd even understand what he meant, somehow.

The musicians flew into a final frenzy as they finished up their first piece, and then Sonny knew it was time to go back to work, no more lazying, even for church. But before he could move on his way, an odd and eerie sensation hit him. A sudden breath of silence seemed to fall over the subway. It was a hush more still than snowfall but not as peaceful. More like the overpowering silence of those moments of staring at the doctor right before he tells you the bad news you already guessed. *It's spread. You're not going to make it.*

That kind of quiet was impossible here; Sonny knew that. The subway was a place of endless trains pulling in, people calling, "Wait," humming to themselves, yelling at each other, one activity rolling loudly into the next all the way through the morning's wee hours and back out the other end. Despite that, it seemed to Sonny that the silence not only existed but grew like a mushroom in humidity, even as a teenage boy dropped coins into the musicians' hat and a gray-haired woman in a fur-collared jacket stopped and bent over to cough, and a thin man with a day's growth of beard rolled in a delivery of newspapers for the underground stand, and an officer near the turnstile stood whistling as he twirled his stick. Sonny saw it all and knew there should be sound but heard nothing, no coins, no cough, no whistling. He felt afraid, like maybe his personal time had arrived, he was in the midst of a stroke or some such. But then he smelled that rank scent that often signaled bad luck coming. A second later, the ceiling began to glitter as though with reflected sunlight, though from where, Sonny couldn't imagine. Sonny doubted anyone else saw it.

Cautionary signs, strong, no denying. He closed his eyes and strained, but he couldn't focus in on the subject of the warning. Still, he had to do something. Though he'd stayed quiet in the past—why risk being picked up as drunk or crazy?—this felt too big. He approached the officer, unable to hear his own footfalls as he walked.

"Officer," he said, "I have hold of a very bad feeling."

"You all right, old man?" The officer moved his face closer to Sonny's. "You need some help?"

Sonny didn't like the "old man" reference, but he felt pleased that when the officer spoke, he could hear the words. Everything else was still silent. "I feel something bad wants to happen, and I hope you keepin' a close eye on everything," Sonny said.

The cop stared at him for a moment and then leaned forward, almost menacing. "What are you talking about?" he asked.

"Police put up signs everywhere," Sonny said. "They say, if you see something, say something."

"Yeah? So what did you see?"

"Not like that," Sonny said. "Just a feeling that won't be leaving me alone. Something not right."

"A feeling." The cop eyed Sonny closely, his eyes dense with suspicion.

"Dangerous today, officer," Sonny said. "I only stopping to tell you to do your job well today because something not right." He felt enormously frustrated that he couldn't be clearer.

Despite that, as soon as he finished speaking, normal noise filled the gap caused by the oppressive silence. As suddenly as it had started, it ended, and Sonny could hear the musicians begin another song, and the conversation of two businessmen who half-ran by, one wearing a tall Russian-style hat, the other saying, "What he's got to learn is . . ." What a relief. Sonny took it as a sign that approaching the officer had been the right choice. He'd done what he could do, and it would help somehow. So he nodded. "Moving on, now," he said. "You'll be taking care of it. You'll be taking care of it." And he began to walk down the stairs to the subway platform.

When he glanced behind one more time, he saw that the cop was already talking on his walkie-talkie, Sonny's tip already being heeded. Something would be done, and he would have been part of it, even if nobody ever knew his name. Another thing to mention to Ruby next time. Already he felt his spirits lift as he took the last couple of steps down the stairs. He boarded a D-train that seemed to hesitate on the tracks, not in a rush despite the rush hour, dawdling as though waiting for him.

NEW YORK: 8:24 A.M.
MECCA: 4:24 P.M.

Vic decided to walk. Clouds scored the sky, and the iciness in the air refused to be ignored. But she didn't feel like taking a taxi. She didn't want anything comforting; she wanted every thing raw and true. Walking briskly, she could probably make it in about twenty minutes. She hoped not to pull any muscles, not today, but she needed to hurry. If he was there in his apartment, where he was, damnit, *supposed* to be—a minor miracle, please, and in return she'd do something to atone for the way she'd doubted him—then she might even make it to rehearsal on time. If he didn't answer the door, she knew where he hid an extra key, taped to the floor under the mat at his front door. She'd go inside, look around. See what he'd left behind.

Though she'd finally really begun to believe that Jonas was missing, she couldn't imagine what that meant exactly. Before leaving her apartment, she went online and typed "missing people" into a search engine. Looking for something almost unnameable: what to do next, how to respond. She clicked on the first website listed, a kind of bulletin board for those searching for loved ones. A twenty-four-year-old girl with hazel eyes, identifying feature a heart-and-moon tattoo on her upper right arm, last seen two years ago in Salt Lake City. A blue-eyed nineteen-year-old boy, vanished from Washington, D.C., almost three years ago. His mother's note: "Luke, if you can, please please just phone and let me know you are okay." A thirty-three-year-old New Orleans man with salt-and-pepper hair, last known to have been planning to attend a church service in Philadelphia, where he had been visiting. His wife was organizing a nationwide "March for the Missing." An entire march. Vic had no idea so many average-looking people had slipped into the ether. She also hadn't yet discovered the ways they might slip back home again. Because some of the stories must end well, surely.

A cold breeze slapped Vic's face. Another of those days when it felt like it would always be winter; she might as well throw away her summer dresses because she would never need them again. Jonas, she suddenly realized, was a child of summer, tall, lanky, blond like a wheat stalk. In the winter, as the city shuttered itself in, it was harder for the heart to keep beating, and especially the heart of a summer being. She would tell Jonas that. She would tell him that what he felt in winter, whatever sorrows or anguish, by spring would be gone.

To her right, a tall building was enshrouded in black—mourning garb, she thought, though she knew it was put in place only to protect the facade until the weather improved enough to allow work to resume. She had to be at the theater, no matter what, by about 11 A.M.; the police were coming there to question her. *The police were coming;* how unlikely that sounded in her own mind. They said it would be brief, but it still required that she offer some explanation to Alex and the rest. And later she needed to see Mara because she owed Mara an apology. And of course this was the last rehearsal day. All these pressing demands just as time felt insistently frozen. Just as it seemed to take forty minutes to put on her coat and mittens and half an hour to walk a measly block. She couldn't remember anymore if she'd seen Jonas's mother yesterday or the day before. The past had become unattractively stuck, like the plastic bags caught in the barren branches in the trees that lined the street. The future: impenetrable. All Vic knew was that she needed to find Jonas so history could start again.

Carol abruptly rose from the couch and saw four sets of eyes shift in her direction: Jake, meeting her glance, turning away, and the three detectives, each with trained, unrevealing gazes, two of them hovering over some kind of high-powered telephone, the third at the window.

"Bathroom," she said, an apologetic explanation, and then slipped from the room.

Locking the door behind her, she sank to the floor. Dear God. How had this happened? Where had she gotten off track? She'd always thought of herself as so attentive. Except for those few months when she'd lost herself in her own Lorenzo-filled life and—*be honest*—considered Jonas only in passing; could that brief period be to blame?

She took a deep breath. Everything was fine; maybe everything was fine. Maybe next week Jonas would forgive her craziness and they would laugh together. *This is the way mother-love works,* she'd explain to him. *There's no controlling it, and there's nothing like it, not the way a cleric loves his God or a soldier his country or a man his wife. This baby emerges, and that's it—you're sucked into a maelstrom so profound you never get out, and so you worry, you overreact sometimes, all you want is to protect your baby. Even if he's shaving now.* Maybe she'd suggest they take a trip together, just the two of them. Jonas liked to camp, and it had been a while since Carol had slept in a tent. Or they could fly to the Caribbean. A beach somewhere.

What she couldn't dismiss, though, was not just the way her jaw felt: rock-like, as if talking would be difficult, smiling an impossibility. It was also how Jake was beginning to look. Afraid, his cheeks blotchy. How could she quiet her own panic when he looked like that?

She felt dizzy, too. She rested her forehead on the heels of both hands. Maybe if she and Jake, together, concentrated very hard. Maybe Jonas would feel that energy and show up, or call, or send a text message. She never prayed—maybe once or twice as a kid, "Now I lay me down to sleep," but not as an adult. But she knelt on the bathroom tile and gripped the white porcelain of the sink. "Oh, my God, please," she said. "Please please please."

Jonas. He taught her humility, the way a child does, and how to love godlike, selflessly. And there was more to learn. She wasn't finished yet.

She heard footsteps outside the door. "Ma'am? You okay?" One of the detectives.

"Out—" Her voice broke. She took a couple of short breaths, trying to steady herself. "Out in a minute," she said.

"Okay, ma'am." But the steps did not retreat.

Was this really *her* life?

She reached to pull a towel off the rack, folded it twice, put it on the floor as padding, and began touching her head repeatedly to the floor. Prostrating herself. "Jonas," she whispered, as though calling to him. "Please, please come home. Come home now. My God. Please, Jonas, my God, please. Please."

She rose abruptly, then, before the words could turn into a wail of a hundred letters that she feared, once begun, would last a hundred days, a hundred years. She hung up the towel, flushed the toilet, ran water in the sink mindlessly. All the while, the word "please" repeated in a loop in her mind, vibrating through her body from her head to her weak knees to the soles of her feet, a never-ending prayer.

NEW YORK: 8:37 A.M.
MECCA: 4:37 P.M.

*"The son will march forth without
permission of the father, the wife without
  permission
of the husband, the debtor
without permission of the creditor."*

A line Jonas had memorized from *The Virtues of
the Jihad*, written in the 1990s by a fervent
Pakistani. An injunction to be buried with the dust
of your struggle still clinging to your coat. He'd
read the pamphlet in the training camp. There'd
also been several lectures about "the Obligation,"
and he and Masoud had discussed the concept. He
found himself thinking of it again now as rush
hour hit New York City. Whispering to himself
like a mantra, the words at once necessary and
almost meaningless. The obligation to look carefully, to admit to yourself what you saw, and
then—no matter how difficult—to act accord-
ingly. Shore up what needed supporting; change
what was false or shallow or dangerously unkind.

He pulled on the clean jeans. The stiff fabric slid
up his slick legs. Though he needed to move
quickly, still he paused for a second to put his fingers at his hips, to feel the solidity of the bones
there, to acknowledge for a moment the beauty of

his own human frame. Then he fastened the top button of the jeans. Still bare-chested, he stepped to the window to look out. Cold but clear. He would not see the season's first snowfall, but while that thought would have created anguish within him a few hours ago, now he noted it simply as an observation.

His ideas, in fact, as well as his emotions, seemed disconnected from him in some essential way. As if he were paddling a canoe and coming upon notions as randomly as rocks in the lake, steering around them so as not to be grounded. Rowing on.

"Insofar as the fire does not enter our home,
we feel we are safe. We pretend, even,
not to feel the heat of the flames
that burn the homes of our neighbors."

Another line from the same pamphlet.

He ran his hands over the smoothness of his chest. He went to the coat closet, which he'd shut tight and left closed after Masoud had left. Now he opened it, reached for the vest, pulled it out on its hanger. He studied the vest a moment, resting his hand on the explosives that would soon nestle against his belly, as if he were bestowing blessings.

Very carefully, he slipped it over his head, onto his sleek body, tugging it down gently in the front so it covered his belly button, reaching to do the same in the back. It fit perfectly.

He hoped matters would not heal seamlessly. He wanted, after all this, nothing short of the collapse of Rome. His mother, and his father, and Vic, and his own memory deserved that much. The world deserved that much. Things had to change. If they didn't change this time, there would simply be more bloodletting. Next year, or a decade from now. It wouldn't stop until it stopped.

He paddled on past that rock, allowing his thoughts to flow freely again. He went to the bathroom and stood in front of the mirror. He verified that his expression held serenity. That was the look that he wanted for the photograph he took of himself reflected in the mirror. Bald, tranquil, with vest. A prayer.

He reached for the shirt Masoud had left him, a white, sack-like, Egyptian-style shirt. No embroidery, no embellishment. He raised his arms above his head and slipped it on. On top of that would go his coat, nothing more, though usually on a day like this one, he would wear a sweater as well. Maybe a down vest, too. Jonas ran to cold. Without those layers, he might be cold, at first, today.

He pulled from his backpack a knitted ski cap, orange. The kind of orange meant to alert hunters to your presence in the woods during deer season. So you don't get shot by accident. It was a new cap, as new as he was now. He'd bought it especially for today. He put it in front of the door, standing up next to the two letters. Organizing the items he wanted to bring as if he were afraid he'd forget them. The orange round and the white rectangular. He snapped a photograph.

He knelt, carefully, on the prayer mat. He wanted to allow his mind a free moment before he headed out the door, because once he headed out the door, he would have to park the canoe, rein in his wandering thoughts, remain focused. He closed his eyes, softened his shoulders, relaxed into the dense blackness of the space between his brain and his shuttered lids. His breathing, he realized, had turned shallow, probably been shallow for hours now. He tried to inhale into his belly, but his belly resisted all unnecessary movement. He would have to accept that. His eyes closed, he pictured his father. Jake was kneeling on the floor in front of Jonas, but not Jonas as he was today; Jonas as a small boy. Jonas the boy lay in bed. Jake rested his hand gently on Jonas's stomach. "My sweet, my precious child," Jake said, and it was so vivid that Jonas was sure he actually heard those words said aloud, in the apartment on the Avenue of the Finest. He could not, though, remember his father ever saying that to him in real life. Jake's tone held a quality of inconsolability. Jonas the boy in the bed sat up and hugged Jake. "I love you,"

Jonas said aloud to his father, to the image of his father. He realized, then, that he hadn't written a letter to his father, and he wondered if he should remedy that, but he felt beyond writing now. Mohammed's father, Abdullah, died six months before the prophet was born. And what had happened to Jesus's earthly father, Joseph? He effectively vanished, as Jonas's father had. Within these absences, the sons forgave. The sons rose to greatness. "I love you," Jonas said aloud again.

Then the vision of his father vanished. Nothing remained but colors, shades of yellow and red.

Eyes still closed, Jonas reached up and touched his parted lips with the fingers of his right hand. Lips were so important. He hoped he'd done enough with his. Said enough. Laughed enough. Meant enough. Kissed enough.

He pressed his hands together, yoga-style, in front of his chest, and bowed his head, eyes still closed. He needed, again, to release his shoulders. He pulled them down, feeling his neck lengthen. He retained all his tension in his shoulders. He probably always would, he thought, and then smiled at the thought. Of course he always would. There wasn't that much *always* left.

He rose. It was time. He knew it without looking at the wristwatch he'd put on the floor next to the bed. He put the Qur'an in the front pocket of his shirt. He stuck one arm, then the other, into the sleeves of his coat, put the letters in his pocket.

The detonator was already there. He pulled his hat onto his head.

He opened the door and then remembered: the nails. The nails were to slip into his coat pocket so he could be as effective as possible when the moment came. They were in a pile on the floor in the corner. Large nails that would be used not to build a chair but to build a house. Two handfuls. One for each coat pocket. He touched the steel point of one to the palm of his hand, imagining for a second a crucifixion. It felt startlingly sharp, an unnecessary insult. No. No, he decided, without more thought than that, and released the nails back into the corner.

Before he left, he took one final searching glance around the studio apartment. A used tea bag and the chipped mug sat on the counter. His skiing pictures remained taped to the wall. The bed cover was rumpled; the prayer rug lay in the corner. Masoud would come claim it, roll it up, perhaps use it himself this very night for evening prayers—a sign of the ongoing connection between the two men.

There were many issues to care about in the world. The environment, education, legal rights for transgendered people. What Jonas cared about was violence, man against man, the imbalance it had created between the powerful and the weak, and the need for somebody who recognized it to even the scale because otherwise the world risked spontaneous combustion, an energy so angry it would engulf itself fully, leaving only ashes behind. One man ending his family name so that others could, eventually, thrive.

Jonas closed the door. He didn't lock it.

On the street, he headed downtown, away from the subway station, opposite the direction that he needed to go. He strode quickly. Carefully, though, because of the vest. He didn't want anyone bumping into him, and the streets were crowded. The streets were crowded, but he couldn't hear anyone talking. He heard only two birds, though he couldn't see them. He imagined them chatting from their perches on neighboring buildings far above his head. And then he passed them, and he heard nothing, as though he'd become Charlie Chaplin skipping through a silent film. "The Tramp" without the hair. He thought of those others who had floated above the world before carrying out their mission, and how the land and people below must have seemed small and even unreal. To be among, instead of above, was after all a braver act.

Three blocks from the Avenue of the Finest, he stopped at a mailbox on the corner he'd spotted the previous day and fished the letters and post-card from his pocket. This box was far enough away that it would not be damaged. He was taking the number 6 up to Grand Central, but downtown, everything would remain intact. His notes would eventually settle in the hands for which they were meant, even if it took an extra day or so because of the ensuing confusion.

Then he turned and walked back the way he'd come. He touched his waist once or twice. He'd begun to hear again, but selectively. Odd combinations of words that slipped from passing mouths. They pulsed through him like blood, but between each phrase fell silence.

As desirable as.
She buried her face in.
Possibly drugged, though I can't say.
My gold bikini and the best shampoo.

He loved it. Jonas loved it all. He knew his breathing had grown even more shallow, and maybe it was making him light-headed, but to him it seemed that the voices and street noises were music, the passersby long-lost neighbors. Some stared at him long enough to discern his kindness and understand his motivation, and then they smiled. He was judged and not found wanting.

At the edge of the steps that led down into the subway, Jonas paused. He raised his head, nose skyward like a hunting dog sniffing the air. He touched his fingers to his waist again and then gripped the cold metal of the handrail with his right hand. It was as if he'd taken hold of a talisman. He felt the metal's worn but dependable sturdiness seep into his muscles, all the way up to his shoulders. He was strong. Stronger than fear.

He pulled his MetroCard from his back pocket and took another shallow breath of the mortal earth's air. And then he stepped into the steady stream of people, was carried with them, by them, down, deep into the subway.

ACKNOWLEDGMENTS

Deepest thanks to: my tireless and generous-hearted agent, Marly Rusoff, and her amazing team, including Julie Mosow and the poetic Michael Radulescu. Fred Ramey for his unmatched wise editing eye, as well as Greg Michalson, Caitlin Hamilton Summie and the entire inspiring Unbridled gang. Blue Mountain Center, as my month ensconced there got me through the first draft. Many early readers, including the very first reader, Susan Ito, and also Arra Hamilton, Caroline Leavitt, Ericka Lutz, Briana Orr, Cheney Orr, Nancy Wall, Amanda Eyre Ward. David Orr for his patient and unwavering support, and Bri, Che and Daylon for more gifts than I can name.

Center Point Publishing

600 Brooks Road ● PO Box 1
Thorndike ME 04986-0001 USA

(207) 568-3717

US & Canada:
1 800 929-9108
www.centerpointlargeprint.com